He leaned in slowly, giving her every chance to pull away, praying all the while she wouldn't.

He brushed his lips softly against hers, then kissed her lightly, only once, the small motion causing every nerve in him to stand on edge.

He wanted so much more, but he would have to be satisfied with this for the time being. Paige needed her space. When she was ready, she would have to make the next move.

But, for the first time in a long time, he felt confident enough, and ready, to try again with a woman. This woman. The frayed edges Callie had left behind seemed to have softened just a bit since he'd met Paige.

On the other hand, if this was what she could do to him after just a few days, he was in real trouble.

Dear Reader,

For much of my life, I've longed to see my name on the cover of a book. The fact that you're now holding *His Texas Forever Family*—my debut novel—in your hands is proof that with a little faith, a little luck and a lot of hard work, dreams really do come true.

I'm a firm believer in second chances, and some of my favorite stories involve characters who must start over after life circumstances toss them around a bit.

Paige Graham has been through major tragedy, but maintaining a fast-paced career while caring for her young son, Owen, has taken a toll on her and prevented her from being able to process her grief, or even consider moving forward. So when Liam Campbell comes along, offering his own unique brand of respite and healing to both Paige and Owen, it takes her a while to accept the idea of a new partner, especially one who has a few bridges to cross himself.

It is my hope that, if you've ever had to make a new start after life's thrown you a curveball, this story brings encouragement.

And, as a new author just spreading my wings, I want to thank you, from the bottom of my heart, for choosing this book.

Very best wishes!

Amy Woods

His Texas
Forever Family

—

Amy Woods

H HARLEQUIN® SPECIAL EDITION®

ISBN-13: 978-0-373-65840-4

HIS TEXAS FOREVER FAMILY

Printed in U.S.A.

HHARLEQUIN®
www.Harlequin.com

AMY WOODS

Although she's wanted to be a writer since learning to read, Amy Woods took the scenic route to her job as an author. She's been a bookkeeper, a high school English teacher, a claims specialist and a call-center worker, but now that she's tried making up stories for a living, she's never giving it up. She grew up in Austin, Texas, and still lives there with her wonderfully goofy, supportive husband and a very spoiled rescue dog. Amy looks forward to getting to know her readers and can be reached on Facebook, Twitter or at her website, www.amywoodsbooks.com.

For Carly Silver,
editor extraordinaire, who believes in my writing
and helped make a lifelong dream come true.

For J.R.—
the crazy guy who married me and taught me
to believe that true love exists, and that
finding happiness is worth taking risks.

For Mom,
whose unwavering love and support allow me to fly
and offer a soft place to land when I fall.

For Maggie—
the rescue dog who stole my heart
and has me wrapped around her little dewclaw.

Chapter One

"Assistant Principal Graham," the intercom spat, "please report to Art Room One. Your assistance is needed immediately."

Paige Graham looked up from the two ten-year-olds she'd just separated from a scuffle and listened as the receptionist called her a second time over the school's outside intercom.

What now?

"This time it's just a warning, but if you two keep this up, we're going to have a talk with your parents," she told the boys.

"Yes, Ms. Graham," the boys said obligingly in unison, though they glared at each other from where they stood on either side of her.

Paige ran a hand through the wind-twisted tangles

of her hair and checked her watch. Only 9:00 a.m.
and the day was shaping up to be an uphill battle.
The first day of school was always hectic, which was
to be expected with the kids still sun-gilded, full of
summer energy and longing to catch up with their
friends. Throughout her career as a school admin-
istrator, she'd had many chaotic first days, but this
one took the cake so far—and the blissful sound of
the last bell was still hours away.

Paige stepped out from between the boys and
made her way from her post near the bus drop to
the front of Peach Leaf Elementary School. Glancing back over her shoulder to make sure the boys'
brawl didn't rekindle in her absence, she stepped inside the glass double doors.

She tossed hellos and welcome-backs to her colleagues as she passed familiar students on her way
down the first-floor hallway to the art classroom.

Why couldn't a teacher with a planning period
look in on the class? Or heaven forbid, a prearranged
substitute teacher?

Then again, it was the first day of school, so it was
entirely possible that all the teachers' aides were occupied helping out with their new classes and didn't
have a spare moment to assist with another. She
could definitely relate.

It was only morning, but Paige already had a
packed schedule—a meeting with her boss, Principal Matthews, in less than an hour, a few special-
education plans to look over and sign before then…
not to mention the new-teacher luncheon and two

afternoon Individual Education Plan conferences. The nature of her job meant a steady stream of unpredictable adjustments and rearranged schedules, but the crammed day ahead left little room for taking over a class at the last minute

Paige cursed herself for wearing her new shoes on the first day of school. She should have worn her trusty low-heeled black pumps with the sensible insoles and not these cute but torturous, toe-pinching, three-inch-high sling-backs before having had a chance to break them in. Why was she trying to follow trends? She was much better off sticking with the black basics and clean lines she usually wore to prove that, despite being only thirty-one, she was indeed serious about her position as assistant principal.

Reaching the art room, Paige opened the door and pulled a deep breath into her lungs.

Although a few students were running around chasing each other, and several others had opened cabinets to pull out crayons and paper, a quick scan of the room indicated that at least nobody was bleeding or seriously injured, and the paints were lined up on a high windowsill in a tidy rainbow. And none of the kids had decided to give each other tattoos—yet.

Paige was surprised at the nervous fluttering of butterflies in her stomach. She'd had several years of teaching experience before she'd landed the coveted Assistant Principal job at Peach Leaf Elementary. She still adored working with kids, but there was no denying that a few years had passed since she'd been on the front line and she wasn't exactly thrilled to be pitched back into it without warning on the first day of school.

Where was he?

Paige tried to recall the new instructor's name. *Something Camden,* she thought—*no*—*Campbell.* That was it: Liam Campbell. He'd been hired by Principal Matthews at the last minute from a school in Abilene on very high recommendation from his former boss, although Paige wondered now why he'd moved if his last school had loved him so much.

"Hey, give that back!" The shout interrupted her thoughts and, squaring her shoulders, Paige stepped farther into the classroom and cleared her throat.

"All right, guys," she said sternly, causing the kids to stop what they were doing and scurry to their desks. Maybe these new heels were a good idea after all. They did add a couple of inches to her petite frame, creating what she hoped was an authoritative presence.

The students paused and turned from each other to stare at Paige, their excited grins disappearing behind tightened lips at her warning tone.

"I see some familiar faces, but for those of you who are new, I'm Assistant Principal Graham."

Paige couldn't help but smile inwardly at the collective intake of breath. There was something cautionary about the word "Principal" that made kids think twice before acting out in her presence. When working with kids, Paige knew she was fair and gentle, but she could also draw a hard line when necessary. And she liked it that way.

She looked out at the room of fifth graders, most of whom had found desks and straightened their spines reflexively against the backs of their chairs when she introduced herself.

"Mr. Campbell is running a little bit late, so we're going to have to be patient until he gets here," she said.

The kids looked around at each other and she caught a few wary glances between friends.

"Does anyone want to talk about what they did this summer?" Paige's question was met with more than a few eye rolls. She had to admit it was a bit routine, but what else could she do when the lesson plan for the day wasn't anywhere to be found? Paige could barely draw a stick figure, much less teach art.

"Somebody must've done something cool or exciting." She looked at a familiar student grinning from the front row. "Katie, why don't you tell us what you did this summer?" As the little girl described her week at the beach and then several other students chimed in with their adventures, the elusive Mr. Campbell finally decided to grace the class with his presence.

Paige released a small sigh of relief, thankful to have escaped the possibility of a boredom-induced mutiny.

"Good morning, class," he said, surveying the room. "I'm your art teacher, Mr. Campbell."

Even as he moved quickly, his posture remained somehow both easy and confident. His slacks and button-down shirt, the large camping backpack slung over one shoulder and the healthy ruddiness of his cheeks made him look like a graduate student back from some exotic archaeological dig rather than a new teacher at a Texas elementary school. Paige wondered again what he was doing in Peach Leaf and what prompted him to move to the small town.

She'd have to be blind not to notice how ruggedly gorgeous the new teacher was. He was so tall that his head had almost made contact with the doorway as he entered. His eyes, the color of pine needles, were set underneath longish, tousled ebony hair and eyebrows, which rose in what looked infuriatingly like humor. And when Liam spoke, those eyes grinned at her, the slightest crinkles at the corners revealing that there wasn't much he took seriously.

Including, it seemed, being on time to the first day of a new position.

Paige was almost grateful for the angry burn rising up in her chest because it made it easier to stop focusing on Liam's dark good looks.

"Well," she said, moving to block him from heading straight to his desk. "Good morning, Mr. Campbell. So glad you're able to finally join us."

A few snickers broke the quiet that had settled upon his arrival.

She knew she should keep her annoyance to herself, especially in front of the kids, but Paige felt the hot itch of irritation in her chest as she watched the new teacher move casually into his new classroom, as though he hadn't arrived late on his first day and wreaked havoc on her carefully planned morning.

"So sorry," Liam said in the West Texas drawl almost everyone in Peach Leaf shared. Somehow, though, his accent was deeper and richer, and it sounded disturbingly warm to Paige.

"Never mind," she told Liam, straightening her spine and pushing her shoulders back. "You've got plenty to do here, as your class is almost over and you've yet to even take attendance. We'll discuss this later."

"All right," Liam said, "and again, my apologies. Perhaps if you knew the reason for my…"

"As I said," Paige interrupted, crossing her arms tighter and glaring at him, "we'll have to speak later. I'm due for a meeting and, well, you have a class to teach."

She released one arm and raised a palm in the direction of the fifteen pairs of eyes staring from the desks. It crossed her mind briefly that she was being a bit hard on him. First days were rough on everyone. But she'd learned from being in charge of kids, including her own son, that it was always better to be firm at first and lay out expectations clearly. The warmth would come later, when they'd figured out it was in their best interest to follow the rules.

"Okay, then. Have it your way," Liam said, one corner of his mouth turned up as though he might laugh at her. She wanted to reach up and knock the grin off his face. How dare he not take her seriously? What could possibly be funny about this situation?

"Good. I'll expect you in my office after the last bell."

Paige ignored the kids' collective "ooh" that followed, but Liam silenced it with a single stern look and a raised hand, and she made a mental note of how he quickly established control in his classroom. He definitely had a strong presence. Maybe he'd make a good teacher yet. He just needed to know what was expected of him.

Especially when her little boy would be in his afternoon class.

Liam nodded and then stared at her for a moment, hands on hips, lips curved up at the corners in what could only be a mocking grin before Paige realized she was blocking the aisle. She took a step aside so he could make his way to his new desk, but Paige couldn't help herself and reached out an arm.

"And Mr. Campbell?" she said, tapping his forearm as he passed.

"Yes," Liam said, turning to look at her.

"Do try to be on time to our meeting."

"Okay, class, that's all for today," Liam told his first graders that afternoon. "Don't forget to bring an object from home tomorrow. We're going to be telling stories about them, and then on Wednesday we'll get to start painting pictures of them. So pick something you really, really like. You'll be stuck with it for a few days so you don't want to choose something you can't stand to look at."

The musical sound of the kids' giggles filled the room as Liam scrunched up his face in mock disgust. He finished collecting the students' drawings and, as they filed out, Liam wiped his face and sunk into his chair, setting his feet on the desktop.

After the unfortunate introduction to the Assistant Principal, he'd been flustered, and it took him a bit before he recalled the lesson he'd planned a few weeks ago. Before today, he'd only met with Principal Matthews, who had hired him. But Assistant Principal Graham was something else—a force to be reckoned with—and he supposed he'd just have to get used to her in time. But he didn't appreciate the way she'd lit into him in front of his students without allowing him to get a word in edgewise in the way of explanation. He planned on telling her so at their meeting in a few minutes.

With her shoulder-length blond curls and her baby blue eyes, she had looked like the human version of a spring day. He loved that she wore so little makeup and he could see fully the fresh glow of her creamy skin—even underneath the red-hot anger that had covered her face. Liam chuckled to himself as he thought of how mad she'd been—so out of proportion to the circumstance. She'd acted for all the world like a fire-breathing dragon and there'd been something about her seriousness that had made him want to push her buttons even more.

Not that he hadn't been in the wrong. Liam never made it a practice to be late to work. In fact, he hated that he'd made a bad impression on his first day, which he'd have to work twice as hard to overcome. It was just that his morning art-therapy group at the hospital where he interned part-time could sometimes draw him in and he found it incredibly difficult to pull away from them, even though he knew the drive back to Peach Leaf would take an hour. Unlike the kids he would be teaching at the elementary school, the kids in the group he'd started as part of his dissertation research struggled with burdens that even their parents had trouble understanding—anything from minor speech impediments to serious emotional baggage caused by various types of trauma. It was Liam's job to teach his patients various methods of expression that would allow them to begin working through their pain.

Helping kids uncover their deepest emotions was the first step to healing. Often art gave them a way to articulate their feelings about whatever distress had brought them to his practice. He could then converse with them about how to feel better. He'd seen all kinds of grief over his years as a certified art therapist and had witnessed the power that making art could have when it came to expression. Many times, his patients didn't even realize what they were feeling until it revealed itself during the repetitive motions of painting or molding clay. It was an amazing thing to watch, and Liam hoped that someday soon, when he'd completed his doctorate, he could explore even further the potential of art in mending broken lives.

But he'd have to make sure to compartmentalize the two to keep from being late again. At least until he could make his dream of becoming a full-time therapist come true.

He did love teaching, especially the first graders who made up his last class of the day. They were still very young and, for the most part, sweet to their teachers and each other, but their minds were eager and fresh and were opening up to the world in ways that were exciting to watch. In the past hour, Liam had loved watching their creative brains at work as they'd begun their first drawings of the year. Seeing students learn about themselves through art was why he'd chosen to teach—at least before his master's classes had introduced him to the captivating possibilities of art therapy. It was during those classes that he'd discovered how powerful self-expression through art could be in helping children understand difficult circumstances like death, illness or divorce—things that, without intervention, could cause enough disruption to stall learning during formative years.

As he walked to his meeting with Assistant Principal Graham, he vowed to make her understand that he loved and respected this job and that he wouldn't be late again. He couldn't risk losing his position if he wanted to stay in Peach Leaf, and he didn't want to go back to his teaching job in Abilene.

At least not while Callie was still working at the school. Not after the way things had ended.

The city and his old job held too many memories. He needed a fresh start, a new beginning where no one knew his old family name, and where he didn't connect moments with Callie to every landmark and street corner. In Peach Leaf, he hoped he could just be Liam Campbell, art teacher—not Liam Campbell, the divorced, black-sheep son of a famous oil tycoon.

When he departed Abilene, he'd left behind his broken heart and had no interest in ever seeing his father or Callie again. He had always wanted kids, but Callie had never taken to the idea. They'd gotten together in college and at that time, Liam hadn't given it much thought because they'd been young. But as the years of their marriage had gone on and she'd resisted the conversation with more vehemence, Liam had eventually let it drop. And then she left him, and from where he sat now, following a messy divorce, he wasn't sure that the possibility of children was anywhere in his future.

No, what he needed now was to look ahead and make his home here, away from the pain he'd left behind, and focus on his career. He refused to let any woman get close to him again—they had no place in his life. And after what had happened with his ex-wife, he was pretty sure they had no place for him either.

Which was why it was so frustrating that Assistant Principal Graham had gotten to him the way she had that morning.

As he neared the front office, Liam tried to push the thoughts of his failed relationship and the fiery assistant principal out of his mind. This past summer had been the roughest of his life, and he was ready for a new beginning. But something else was crowding his mind. He needed to talk to her about the interesting student in his last-period class. At first the kid hadn't stood out to him at all; if anything, he'd blended in a little too well, being much quieter and far more reserved than a typical first grader.

But he did eventually stick out. The kid had been completely silent and hadn't said a single word the entire class, while the others had been chatty little balls of energy. The students had all readily offered their names, wiggling in their seats as they'd raised their hands for a chance to talk and had interacted with him without any effort.

Except this one.

When Liam had taken attendance, the kids who seemed to be his friends told him the boy's name—Owen. Liam hadn't thought much of it—he knew firsthand from his group that some kids just took longer to come out of their shells, and pushing too hard could have a negative effect. But he'd make a point of talking to Owen tomorrow. And in the meantime, Liam would see if Ms. Graham knew anything about the little guy so Liam could give the boy extra resources if necessary. When he finished meeting with her, he'd go back to his classroom and check his student files to make sure he hadn't missed anything.

"Good afternoon," Liam said as he approached the brunette at the desk in the front office.

The young woman removed her headset and grinned up at him.

"Good afternoon to you," she said, her voice soft and kind, a complete contrast to the low, angry tone—practically a growl—that Assistant Principal

Graham had greeted him with that morning. The voice he couldn't get out of his head.

"And who are you?" He reached his own hand across the receptionist's desk and shook the one she offered.

"I'm Liam Campbell. I have a meeting with Assistant Principal Graham at four o'clock…" Liam looked at the nameplate on the desk, "…Emma," he added.

"Of course," she said, checking her computer. "She's got you down right here. I'll just call her and let her know you'll be in." Emma smiled up at him as she picked up the phone.

"Go on in," she said after a moment.

"She can be a little bit bristly, can't she?" Liam said in a low voice, winking at Emma. Emma giggled and pointed to the short hallway behind her desk. Liam found the door marked "Paige Graham" and tapped softly on the wood.

After a moment, Paige opened the door. Liam cursed himself for the heat that rushed up his spine when he saw her. *It must just be my nerves.* After all, he wasn't exactly looking forward to being chastised again like a troublesome kid. He'd already gotten the point.

She was a prickly one, but dang if she wasn't lovely, too. Her skin glowed in the afternoon light filtering in through the large office windows, and she'd taken off her suit jacket, revealing long, slender arms. As he met the harried expression on her face, Liam found himself thinking that maybe he'd just have to get through a few of her cactus spines before he could find the soft flesh underneath....

Liam stepped past Paige and she closed the door, motioning for him to sit in one of the chairs in front of her desk.

"Is something amusing, Mr. Campbell?" she asked.

He cut short his study of her as she spoke. "Of course not," he said. He hadn't even known he was smiling until she'd caught him. Where was his usual controlled nonchalance?

"Good," she said, briefly returning her attention to the papers spread out on the solemn-looking oak desk.

The desk suits her, Liam thought as he sat and folded his hands on his lap, waiting for her to finish sorting the work that was obviously more important than him.

"Now, Mr. Campbell," she said, finally meeting his eyes. "I won't take too much of your time as I'm sure you have plenty to do," she said, lacing her fingers in front of her. Liam got the strong sensation that he was just another item to check off her To-Deal-With list.

"But," she continued, "I just wanted to make it absolutely clear that tardiness will not be tolerated at this school."

Liam winced at the word. *Tardy?* He wasn't one of her students and certainly didn't appreciate being treated with such disdain. He had a master's degree in art education, *thank you very much,* and was well on his way to a Ph.D., so who was she to talk to him so condescendingly? Sure, she was in a position of authority, but that didn't give her the right to berate him for one mistake. *He* was the one doing the school a favor by filling an open position at the last minute, not the other way around.

Liam set his mouth to keep from saying something he'd regret. Forcing a polite smile, he met her cornflower eyes and addressed her, matching her less than friendly tone with his own.

"As I said this morning, Mrs. Graham, I'm very sorry that I was late. It will not happen again. But there's a good reason…"

"It's *Ms.*, not *Mrs.*, Graham," she interrupted.

He couldn't believe that she wouldn't let him talk for one minute… Wait a second—why was he relieved at the correction? And anyway, what was he doing thinking about her like that? Even if he was interested in letting another woman into his life, which he wasn't, it sure wouldn't be someone as uptight as Paige Graham.

Liam said nothing, concentrating his effort on stopping the cascade of disconcerting thoughts. She'd have to learn to listen before he'd waste another breath trying to talk to her. He was patient, but a man had only so much courtesy, and she was pushing it.

Paige's face softened slightly. "Look, Mr. Campbell, there's something else I want to say." She raised a hand to rub her temples and closed her eyes for a few seconds. The brief gesture caused an unwelcome softness to swell in his chest. He saw for the first time how stressed she seemed to be and noticed the pale purple half-moons under her otherwise pretty— more than pretty, *beautiful,* if he was honest—eyes. After all, she looked barely twenty-five, although Liam assumed she had to be older than that to have worked her way up to her position. She certainly behaved like someone older.

What in her life could possibly account for that air of severity hovering around her?

After a few minutes, Paige opened her eyes and met Liam's, which, despite everything, weren't filled with the irritation she'd expected. She hadn't meant to be so hard on him that morning, and honestly, she owed him an apology. She resisted the urge to explain herself, not wanting to bring up Owen or the challenging time she'd had getting him to school that morning.

It had been her husband's job to get Owen to school most mornings because Paige had to be there so much earlier than her son. It was hard enough on both of them now, with her working at her own child's school, but it had been a lot less stressful when Owen's dad had taken care of getting him there.

A lot of things had been easier when Mark had been around. When he'd been alive.

The past six months had stretched Paige's nerves as thin as they could go. But no matter how hard things had gotten, and no matter how many days and nights she worried how her son would fare growing up without his father, she knew it was always a thousand times worse for Owen. Her heart ached for her little boy, and as she worried about him for the millionth time that day, she had to fight the tears that crowded behind her eyes and threatened to make her look even more off-kilter than she must have already that morning.

But Liam Campbell didn't need to know any of that.

She only needed to reestablish her authority as his superior, and then hopefully she could refer him to Principal Matthews if any issues came up in the future.

She met Liam's eyes, the rich, heady green of them hitting her all over again.

"What I wanted to say is that I'm very sorry for the way things happened this morning."

Paige looked down at her hands. She felt the entire day sitting heavily on her shoulders, and the startling thought invaded her mind of how great a massage would be. How wonderful Liam's large hands would feel, kneading the tension from her tight muscles, melting away the weight of all the hats she wore—assistant principal, mother *and father*. She felt heat rush to her cheeks.

What is wrong with you? Get it together, Paige. You're the man's boss, for goodness' sake.

"Even though it was unprofessional and inconvenient of you to arrive late on your first day, I shouldn't have reprimanded you in front of the kids, and I do apologize."

Despite her intention, it didn't sound like much of an apology, even to her own ears. She hoped he would accept it anyway. What was it about him that set her off so easily, that made her want to keep him at a safe distance from the rush of confusion in her body, yet also draw him nearer?

"That's fine," Liam said, offering her a gentle smile that Paige hoped was as sincere as she'd meant her words to sound. The last thing she needed was to be at odds with one of her staff. Their opinions of her meant more than most of them probably knew, especially with the possibility of a promotion coming up.

She'd been a teacher herself after graduating from college until she finished her master's degree and became a supervisor two years before, so Paige knew exactly what instructors went through each day on the job and how tough it could be sometimes. She made a point to visit her staff in action regularly and talk with them so that she didn't lose touch with what it felt like to be in the classroom.

"So, then," she said, feeling relieved. "Can we start fresh? Consider this our first meeting?"

Paige hoped she didn't sound too desperate. Something about this man just put her on edge. Liam looked at her, his eyes still narrowed a little—trying to read her, she supposed—and then seemed to decide it was safe to agree to a truce. He reached a large hand across her desk. She noticed the colors underneath his fingernails and caught the pleasant, familiar scent of crayon wax from his skin and thought of how much Owen loved art. She resisted the strong compulsion to ask how Liam's first day of class had gone, and whether or not he'd noticed her son's disability.

"Done," he said. Paige shook his hand and started at how wonderful it felt, firm and warm around her own small, cool one. She hoped he didn't notice her slight jump at his touch and was grateful when he quickly pulled away from her and rose to leave. He made it to the door and turned back around to retrace his steps, and her heart did a small flip.

"I wanted to ask you about one more thing," he said, sitting back in the chair and resting his elbows on his knees.

"Of course."

"There's a young man in my last class, the first graders, who I noticed has a bit of an issue. With all the first-day stuff, the period went by fast, so it could be nothing, but I wanted to make sure. I thought you might know if there's a history."

A lump rose quickly in Paige's throat, and she could feel her neck turning crimson with heat. She knew instantly he was talking about Owen and was thankful Liam hadn't made the connection. After all, Graham was a fairly common surname, and the new teacher had so many new names to commit to memory that he'd likely overlooked it.

She looked up to see his brows knit with concern— concern for her child.

"Is everything okay?" he asked, leaning forward to place a hand on her desk.

"Yes," she lied.

Paige willed herself to maintain composure. She was an assistant principal and every kid should be her priority. She couldn't think of Owen any differently.

But he was different. He was her own. And things were obviously still not okay, even after everything they'd tried over the past six months to get him talking again. She'd known she'd been senselessly optimistic by hoping that Owen's first day of first grade would miraculously cure his selective mutism, but her heart had jumped ahead anyway and she hadn't been able to stop herself from hoping he might speak to his friends or his new teachers.

Despite the rocky time they'd had getting to school that morning, Paige had been hoping that they could both start fresh this year.

That the Owen she knew would recover and resume communicating with the rest of the world.

But nothing had changed, and Paige had to admit they were running out of options.

She snapped back to her office. Liam was staring at her, his green eyes full of curiosity.

She would have to find the right way to bring up Owen. As a parent of one of his students, she knew there would come a time soon enough when Liam would find out about Owen's disability, but Paige didn't want him to think her incapable of objectivity by focusing all of her attention on her own son at their first one-on-one meeting. As assistant principal, all of the students were her responsibility, not just her own little guy.

"What is it?"

"Well, it could just be that it's the beginning of the year, and the boy is shy, but..." Liam hesitated.

"But..." Paige prompted.

"But he didn't speak during the whole period. I mean, he didn't say a single word. And, like I said, maybe it's just first-day jitters. We've all had that, including me, but..."

Paige ignored the reference to their morning run-in.

"Even with all of that, most first graders I know have plenty to say, and well, this kid didn't say anything. It seemed like more than just shyness. I think there might be something more serious going on."

Paige forced herself to swallow the fist-sized lump in her throat before working up the courage to speak, and she sent up a silent wish that her voice would come out sounding as normal as possible.

"I'm just curious, so that I can look into finding extra help for him if it comes to that, but may I ask something?" Paige said.

Liam nodded.

Paige measured her words carefully, wanting desperately to know every single detail about what had gone on during the class, every minute piece of information possible but knowing too that it was her job to give Owen the chance to be a normal kid. To let his actions, rather than her overprotective nature, speak for him. She knew he would hate it if he found out that she'd been talking to Mr. Campbell. And she couldn't stand feeling that she'd betrayed her son.

"Did the other kids make fun of him or tease him in any way? Did they seem to think there was something…wrong…with him?" If Liam picked up on her hesitation to be frank with him, his face gave nothing away. He seemed to simply weigh her question carefully before answering with equal mindfulness.

"No, nothing like that. And actually, Owen seems to have quite a few buddies in the class. But when I tried to get him to talk to me, even to introduce himself, he wouldn't interact at all. Some of the others even spoke up for him, which is kind, but, in reality, can sometimes make situations like his even worse."

"Situations like his?" Paige asked. Had Liam met other children with something like Owen's condition? In her years of teaching, she'd seen similar conditions a couple of times, but for those kids it had always passed as the school year went on and they made friends. For Owen, it didn't seem to be improving despite six months of behavioral therapy. Even though Dr. Roberts knew the cause, he hadn't yet been able to get Owen to talk to anyone besides his mother.

"Well, yes. I've seen it a few times actually. Both in my teaching experience and in…"

Liam was interrupted as Paige's office door opened and a small, sandy-haired boy burst in, stopping just inside as his blue eyes shot back and forth between the two adults who had turned to stare at him.

"Well, hi there," Liam said, smiling at the child.

"Hi, sweetie," Paige said, unfreezing her limbs and rising quickly from her chair. "Come on in."

"Mr. Campbell," she said, "I think you've already met my son, Owen."

Chapter Two

Paige took a deep breath, put a hand on her son's shoulder and squeezed it gently.

"Owen, say hello to Mr. Campbell. He's the new art teacher. You met this afternoon in class."

Owen said nothing but looked up at Liam and reached out a small hand. He seemed to know instinctively that the adults had been talking about him, and Paige resisted the urge to reassure him that he wasn't in trouble. It was important, the therapist had told her at their weekly meetings, to try to let Owen make his own decisions about interactions, to let him be uncomfortable at times, that the silence would at some point naturally urge him to speak. Paige had her doubts about that, but what else was there to do? If Dr. Roberts, who came highly recommended by people Paige trusted, couldn't help Owen, then who could?

"Hi there, Owen," said Liam. He offered a gentle grin and, rising from his chair, reached out to shake Owen's suddenly trembling hand.

"That was some dragon you started this afternoon." Liam's eyebrows rose in admiration. The corner of Owen's lips turned up, ever so slightly, at his new teacher's compliment. "I've never seen such a great dragon before, and I can't wait until it's finished."

Paige glanced at Liam over her son's head as tender gratefulness filled her. Instead of pushing Owen to talk, or asking incessant questions despite the child's silence, Liam simply treated him like a normal kid. Usually Owen was wary around new people, but somehow this man had caused her child to give a hint of a smile. But Paige told herself to stop thinking down that line. She should know by now not to wish for miracles for Owen.

Owen let go of Liam's hand. He looked up at his mother as if asking her what he was supposed to do next, the familiar nervousness and desire to retreat into himself returning to his eyes. Paige squeezed his shoulder again and knelt down so she could look directly at him.

"Owen, why don't you go out to see Emma and keep her company while I finish talking to Mr. Campbell? I won't be long, and she has some new coloring books in her bottom drawer for you." Owen's shoulders relaxed with relief as he gripped the straps of his small red backpack. Paige put a hand on his back and nudged him out the door. She pressed the intercom and asked Emma to watch her son for a few moments.

Liam, still standing, lifted his hands, palms up. In his green eyes Paige saw the pity she found over and over in people's faces when they discovered what Owen was going through. It never got any easier to stomach.

"Do you want to talk about it?" Liam asked.

A million conflicting emotions flooded through her. So he had noticed Owen's silence, and seemed aware that it wasn't just shyness or first-day nerves. Part of her admired Liam for that. A less observant teacher might have overlooked it completely, but this one had caught it on the first day in only an hour's time. He must have more substance to him than his actions thus far had indicated.

On the other hand, she struggled to separate "mom" from "assistant principal," though she knew she'd have to in order to talk about her son with his new teacher.

Paige shook her head and crossed her arms. The comfort she'd felt only a few moments ago vanished completely and she struggled for the right words to describe the complexity that was Owen's selective mutism. Most people had trouble understanding how and why a child who had always been verbal could just stop talking, and their comments, though well meaning, could be hurtful.

"I would, actually—yes—but I don't want you to

treat Owen any differently from any other child just because he's my son."

Paige hesitated, alternating between feeling a desire to unburden herself and wanting Liam to take his sympathy and leave. "Mr. Campbell..."

"Liam," he corrected.

"...Liam. It takes time for most teachers—and most people, for that matter—to even notice that Owen doesn't speak to anyone but me. He tends to keep to himself and blend in. I admire that you were able to pick up on it so quickly. No doubt I judged you, and your teaching abilities, too quickly, but I'd appreciate if you'd think of Owen no more or less than any other child in your classes."

"I get it," he said, moving toward the door. "It's the first day of school and it's understandable."

The kind concern left his eyes and for some reason he seemed to bristle at her words. His body visibly tensed, as though he felt insulted.

"I can assure you that Owen will receive no special treatment from me on account of who his mother is."

Paige nodded. Each time she'd interacted with Liam, awkward tension seemed to arise, and she wished she could erase it. "But," he said, the words lilting softly with his gentle West Texas drawl, "it's mighty important to me that you know that my tardiness this morning will not be a regular thing, and I apologize. I'm very much looking forward to working with the kids and I want you to know that I take this job seriously."

He hesitated as he watched her face closely, his

green eyes searching hers. He took a step closer to her, and though he remained at a respectable distance, a strange shiver ran up Paige's spine.

"And you can trust *me*," he added

Despite his kindness toward Owen, Paige didn't want to trust Liam Campbell. Even trustworthy men, like Mark, could be taken from you at the drop of a hat. She stepped forward and opened the door for him.

As he walked out, Liam met her eyes. Paige wondered if she would ever be able to look at him without her silly heart skipping over his incredible handsomeness. It would be pretty inconvenient if not.

"Listen," he said. "About Owen…if you ever need to talk about what's going on with him—strictly teacher to assistant principal, of course—I'd be glad to discuss it further with you. I have some experience in childhood therapy, and I'd be happy to share it with you."

Paige shook her head. "That's kind of you, but unless Owen has a problem in class or he's not getting work done that he needs to, I think I've got it under control. He has a therapist who we're both working with and, well, the man's supposedly the best there is."

But the best hadn't been good enough to help her son so far. At what point was she going to admit that Owen might never speak to anyone besides her again? What if her nightmare came true and he caved further into himself and stopped speaking altogether, even to her? When would she be able to admit, to herself and to everyone else, that he just wasn't getting better?

Paige didn't want to think about that now.

"Okay, then," said Liam. "I'll let you know if anything comes up."

"Thank you," she said, trying to smile reassuringly. Most of the time there seemed enough of her to go around, but only just. Paige's mother had raised Paige and her sister alone when their father had left. So Paige could manage, too. She'd have to, after the loss of Mark.

She had to admit, though, that she was curious about what experience Liam might have with Owen's disorder. On any other day, she would have allowed Liam to speak more about it. But right now, Paige wanted nothing more than to simply rest her muscles in a boiling hot bath, then curl up on the couch with Owen—and maybe a glass of red wine, which was an indulgence she rarely allowed herself, but one she could sure use today.

Paige collected Owen, agreeing to let him take home one of the coloring books that Emma kept for family conferences. Owen grabbed the book and his backpack, and they made their way out to Paige's old blue pickup.

"Hey, Owen, want to stop at Barb's for dinner?" she asked, as they stepped out of the air-conditioned school and the warm summer afternoon wrapped itself around them.

Owen's blue eyes widened and he nodded his head vigorously at the name of their favorite diner. Once settled in the car, they headed toward Main Street, the August heat dancing in shimmery waves across the asphalt. They both averted their eyes when they passed their old house, which Paige and Owen had shared with Mark as a family. She tried to ignore the urge to pull into the driveway and settle back into her old life. As much as she might wish it, Mark would not be in the backyard, grilling burgers on his day off, or waiting in the kitchen for her with a glass of wine, ready to listen to her talk about her day at work. That life was gone now.

She and Owen had done their best to remain in the house for as long as possible after Mark's death. Paige had been concerned that if they moved, any remaining stability that Owen had in his tumultuous life at that time would have vanished just like his father, so she'd kept the house and had kept Owen from knowing how tight the walls felt around her. She'd kept to herself how hard it was for her to live there. But eventually, to her relief, Owen had asked Paige if they could leave the house and she'd agreed.

The house was large and beautiful, almost as old as the town of Peach Leaf itself, and had been in Mark's family for years. It had been a gift from his grandmother when she and Mark had married, and they'd accepted it with the starry, hopeful eyes of newlyweds before they'd realized what went into maintaining such a place. Paige had grown tired of cleaning it, refusing to hire a housekeeper for something she was perfectly capable of doing on her own, but it had been home, and they'd loved it like the family member it was.

At least until Mark's death.

Paige could still recall the way her heart had dropped straight to the bottom of her chest that night. The doorbell had chimed as she'd finished clearing the dinner dishes and she'd opened it to find Fire Chief Garcia and one of Mark's colleagues standing on her front porch. She'd barely been able to focus on the chief's words as he'd gone over the details of the incident and Mark's success at retrieving an infant, before he died of smoke inhalation.

She shuddered at the memory.

When she and Owen decided to move away from the house, she'd walked through each room, lingering for long moments to store the place in her memory. And now each time they passed, she wondered if they'd ever be free of their loss. If they would ever be able to rebuild as a family.

After dinner, which consisted of Barb's incredible fried chicken and a dessert of homemade vanilla ice cream, made even sweeter by the red vinyl bar stools and black-and-white checkered tiles that Owen loved so much, they headed home, or at least what had passed for home for the past six months.

As Paige drove, Owen chatted about his first day, and her heart did an unwelcome little flip when he mentioned his new art teacher. It seemed Liam Campbell had occupied both their minds all day, whether she liked it or not.

They arrived home to their condo, which was just outside of town and close enough to work that when the weather was nice, they could bike to school together. Paige did the best she could to spend as much time as possible with her son. Though she often wondered if her career was too stressful at this time in her life, she enjoyed her position and especially loved being around the kids. It was a good job and it allowed Owen to have what he needed. She just wasn't sure anymore what exactly it was that he *did* need, and, the longer he went without speaking to others, she was losing hope in her ability to provide it.

Her thoughts wandered again to Liam as she got ready for bed, and she tried not to dwell on his offer to discuss Owen. She didn't need another person to make promises and offer new ideas or treatments. They'd all had enough, and it was getting to the point where Paige was beginning to accept that this was just going to be their life.

The next day at school, Paige avoided Liam. All they'd had was a simple, professional exchange… there was no need to deal with him any further today, unless something came up with Owen.

So why, then, could she not stop thinking about him? There was the part about him being incredibly good-looking. But what was it that kept him on her brain through her morning conferences, through phone calls with parents and through her break? Unfortunately, she had the teacher meeting at three that afternoon, just after school let out. She would have to be chatty with everyone, Liam included.

When Paige arrived at the assembly, the cafeteria was pulsing with teachers milling about, sharing stories from their summer just like the kids had the day before. Paige wondered if anyone else had heard the rumors swirling that Principal Matthews was thinking of retiring

There had been a time when Paige would have loved to take over the position, but after Mark's death, when she'd suddenly turned into a single parent, she had put the thought of becoming principal out of her mind. Besides, she probably didn't have enough experience to get Principal Matthews's job, and there were plenty of teachers who had been working at the school far longer than she. Still, Paige couldn't help mentally crossing her fingers on the off-chance that she had a shot.

Sure, it would be difficult. For one, it would mean even longer hours and less time with Owen. But, on the other hand, it would mean that Owen could get better care if it was available. Dr. Roberts regularly suggested an after-school therapy group of kids Owen's age at their Wednesday meetings. Paige had been seriously considering it but adding more therapy was costly, and the additional hours were not covered by Owen's medical insurance.

She found a seat at an empty table as the last of the staff began to file into the cafeteria. Paige had always struggled to socialize with her employees at gatherings like these, feeling as insecure as a student again. She was expected to behave a certain way as an assistant principal, and she should maintain a certain distance between herself and the faculty, although she'd spent years teaching with many of them.

Despite her position, Paige still considered them

equals, and many of them would always be her friends. But she'd made the decision when she'd first accepted this position that it was better to remain distant from all of them at such events rather than to have anyone thinking that she favored certain individuals.

It was better to be alone.

The cafeteria was full of staff when Liam arrived that afternoon, but he didn't recognize a single face. He really did need to make an effort to leave his classroom more and at least make an attempt to get out of his shell to make friends with his new colleagues. He and Callie had had a wide social circle in Abilene, and he missed getting together with friends. He guessed he would just have to make new ones…eventually.

Another unpleasant side effect of their painful divorce.

His eyes scanned the crowd for anyone he might have met, even briefly. He'd been hired late in the summer, but even in the few summer professional development days he'd attended, he had been too interested in learning the workings of a new environment to do more than share a few words with anyone.

Just as he decided to be the first to occupy one of the empty tables at the back, he caught the enchanting sunny glow of Paige's headful of curls. Liam knew he was acting like a damn fool as he gravitated toward her, but by the time he could do anything about it, she'd caught him coming and it was too late to turn around.

"Hi there," he said, taking a seat on the opposite side of the table at the far end—where there was no *way* she'd get the wrong impression. He had no intention of bothering her. Plus, he didn't think he could stand to hear her inform him yet again how little she needed his help.

In his career, he had seen many parents who wrestled with the idea of alternative therapy like the kind in which he specialized. Generally, he dealt with them at the stage in which they were open to such an idea. Paige wasn't there yet, but against his better judgment, he was finding it awfully hard to resist the urge to persist and recommend that she bring Owen to his hospital sessions. He knew it was selfish, but helping Owen would inevitably equal more time with Paige, a thought that became more appealing each time he caught sight of her. He hadn't wanted it, but he couldn't ignore his growing attraction to the woman.

She greeted him with a tense smile, her eyes working to focus on him as though she'd been distracted.

"Hi, Mr. Campbell," Paige said, moving quickly to pick up her pen. She busied herself flipping through the packet of papers in front of her.

Liam didn't correct her this time. He'd figured out that she preferred the distance of last names when it came to addressing faculty. If he had to guess, it probably made her feel like less of the teacher she'd likely been before she moved to her current position and more like a boss. He'd had plenty of administrators like her in his time, but, for some reason, this one didn't make him want to run in the other direction. In fact, she had the opposite effect, which he wasn't keen to admit. He had no business circling the assistant principal like a bee to honey.

Yet, there he was, at her table in a cafeteria filled with empty ones.

"I don't really know anyone yet, so I guess you're the unlucky tablemate of the new kid," he said as he slid down the table toward her.

Liam was surprised when Paige laughed, the melodic sound tickling his ears and spine. She looked up from her notes and the violet-blue of her eyes glittered at him. It was the first time he'd seen this softer side of her, and he wanted more. What would it take to get her to smile at him like that again and again? Whatever it was, he would do it in a heartbeat.

"I don't mind much. No matter how long I've been here, I always still feel a little like a newbie," she said.

Liam returned her smile. "I would think that in your job, you'd know everyone."

Paige looked down at her papers again and Liam instantly wanted her eyes back on him.

"I suppose in a way I do, but it's difficult being in my position. It puts certain…expectations…on my interactions with other teachers."

Immediately after speaking, Paige bit her full bottom lip, as though she'd said too much. She shook her head a little and put on what looked like an attempt at a confident grin.

"But I love my job. I really do. It's just that… well…" She shook her head and looked up at him again. "I guess every position has its rough spots, doesn't it?"

Liam nodded, hoping he could reassure her. He realized once again that he'd go pretty far to get her to smile at him again, to see those berry lips part one more time and her eyes crinkle around the corners.

With force, he pulled his gaze away from her mouth and met her eyes.

"That it does," he said. "But I love my job, too. It's one of the hardest jobs in the world but also..."

"The best," Paige filled in.

Liam laughed. "Yes, it is pretty great. I've wanted to work with kids in some capacity since I was one myself, and I've always loved art."

Paige grinned and Liam noticed a hint of mischief this time.

"So were you like me, then, with dolls circled around your bedroom waiting with eagerness to hear every word you had to say?"

She was teasing him, he realized, though it felt strange coming from the person who'd been so tense just the previous afternoon. But she was also irresistible.

"Not dolls. Army men," he said.

Paige laughed again. This time, her mouth opened fully and, before he could stop himself, his mind wandered into the dangerous territory of what it would feel like to have his lips against hers.

He really needed to make some friends—male ones. He was way out of line thinking this way about anyone right now, especially about his boss.

"Ah, I see. Army men, then. Same thing."

"Not the same," Liam retorted, frowning in mock seriousness.

Maybe there was more to the dragon lady than met the eye. Maybe she did have a soft underbelly.

Maybe he could get her to show him more of it.

"Did you always want to be a teacher, then?" she asked.

Liam nodded. "Yes, ma'am. Although grad school's opened up some new doors, and now I'm working toward a doctorate in art therapy while I teach."

Though his father had laid it on thick from the beginning that he disapproved of Liam's career choice. It had interfered with the man's plans for his only son—plans that existed prior to Liam's birth and about which Liam had never had a say. His dad had always wanted Liam to go into the family oil business, and Liam's open disinterest in the company had done nothing to dissuade the man. He'd pushed and pushed until Liam hadn't had any option but to push back even harder by flat-out refusing to take over when the time came for his father to retire.

"I'm impressed," Paige said, raising her eyebrows.

"I don't think there's anything out there like working with kids. You get access to these great little brains that are just starting to form ideas and perspectives about the world. And you get to watch them process it every single day and see the way their eyes light up when they've worked really hard and they finally understand. It's really something, if you ask me."

Liam looked up to find Paige watching him intently, and he felt silly. He always got a little mushy when he talked to people about his job.

"I'm sorry," he said, "I just really have a passion for it." Almost unlike anything else. But since starting grad school and spending time with the kids in his art-therapy classes, he'd decided that, ultimately, becoming a full-time therapist was the best path for him. Both teaching and art therapy offered so many promising avenues for children to heal and process grief, but as soon as he completed his doctoral studies and the internship, he would set up a full-time practice of his own.

"I think that's great, actually," Paige said, interrupting his thoughts. "I wish we could find more like you. The kids need people with that kind of passion and interest in them."

"And I think my favorite medium is a great way to get to know them on a deeper level. Kids will do a lot of things with art that they can't do anywhere else."

"What do you mean?" asked Paige. She'd leaned closer to him across the table and she was staring at him, her blue eyes intense under furrowed brows.

"I just mean that art is one of the best forms of communication." Tentatively, he added, "It's also the best way, sometimes, for people to heal." At that, Paige scooted back a little and her eyes darkened. "Did I say something to offend you?"

"No, no," she said, shaking her head. "It's just that word—'healing.'"

"What do you mean?"

"It's nothing. I just seem to find myself thinking more and more about what it actually means for someone to be healed from something."

Liam knew he was getting closer to the core of Paige's discomfort, whatever it might be. He guessed it must be related to Owen's condition. It wasn't a normal thing for a kid to completely stop talking, not unless there was real trauma at the bottom of it. His first thought had been that maybe there was an abusive father in the picture, but Paige had been very clear that she was a Ms., not a Mrs., so possibly that was out—at least he hoped it was.

But he couldn't figure out what else it might be. Usually, children didn't have such reaction to normal, everyday kid problems. It wasn't like a bruise that would gradually heal itself, transitioning from black to purple to yellow, before it simply disappeared. Selective mutism was almost always a response to something very far out of the ordinary. Regardless, Liam knew it couldn't be anything good, and, for some reason, he felt compelled to find out what may have caused it.

The truth was, he had something different to offer Paige and Owen—in the form of art therapy, of course. Liam figured Paige wouldn't be open to it at first. Most parents he worked with had trouble understanding how art could help their children process their emotions. But maybe, just maybe, if he worked slowly to convince her, he could help her son get better. As it was, Owen was probably missing out on social experiences in his formative years. In fact, Liam estimated that, if the boy didn't make major progress soon, resulting emotional damage could last beyond his elementary school years.

Liam could tell easily that Paige was a good mom—a great one, in fact. He knew, though, that often parents were so close to their kids that they lost the ability to see any alternative ways to help them. It was as though they'd sunk into an ocean of advice and needed to be pulled above water again to breathe and start fresh. As a teacher, it was his duty to help each child.

And his desire to help Owen had absolutely nothing to do with the ridiculously lovely Paige Graham.

Before Paige had a chance to say anything more, a microphone crackled up on stage. Principal Matthews addressed the staff, then a barbecue was laid out, filling the air with its rich, enticing scent, and Liam and Paige joined the long line of teachers to get their plates.

Paige knew she should have been mingling with a few teachers, but she had gotten sidetracked...by Liam. It was unnerving how easily he seemed to grab her attention. He was so close that she couldn't concentrate on anything else but his presence behind her. She needed to watch out; otherwise she'd be entering territory she wanted to stay as far away from as possible. Even though six months had passed since her husband's death and she truly wanted to move on at some point, the idea of letting Mark go completely was new enough to frighten her. Taking a step in that direction would be a risk she wasn't yet certain she should take.

As Liam filled his plate, Paige headed off to grab a cup of sweet tea. Despite the delicious aroma that initially caused her mouth to water, and the passing plates piled high with some of her favorite dishes, she somehow wasn't hungry anymore. And she needed to get back to work.

She circulated around the room, armed with her tea, and greeted all the new teachers before catching up with some of the more seasoned ones, many of whom had been close friends when she'd been in the classroom herself. She found herself relieved to be free of Liam for a few minutes. Something about him drew her in. Something comfortable and safe that had her stomach churning with uneasiness—a warm feeling she hadn't had in a long time.

Sometimes she wondered if she'd ever really had a chance to grieve her husband's death, so obsessed had she been with making sure Owen had everything he needed. Mark dying from the fire had been unexpected and traumatic—like something out of a shocking news story that could never actually happen to her.

Paige lost her train of thought as Principal Matthews approached. "How's everything going?" she asked.

"Pretty well. I think I've managed to say at least a few words of encouragement to just about everyone. I think we'll have a good year. You've hired an excellent staff, as usual," Paige said, smiling in appreciation.

"I'm glad," Principal Matthews said. Paige had known the older woman for many years and had admired her just as long. Her silver hair and round, pink cheeks gave her a grandmotherly appearance that kids naturally warmed to. Kind and fair, and always quick to smile at the children, she defied all stereotypes of what kids thought a principal should be. Ms. Matthews had a grandmotherly air about her and the students seemed to think that it would be worse to disappoint her than to be shouted at by her. If Ms. Matthews would indeed be retiring soon, her shoes would be very hard to fill. Paige couldn't imagine anyone doing the job as well.

"Paige," Ms. Matthews said, reaching up to place a small hand on her shoulder. "There is something I'd really like to talk to you about if you have a moment tomorrow afternoon."

"Yes, of course." Paige hoped she hid her sudden concern. She couldn't guess what it might be, but she knew there had been an incident with a student's parents that morning. Apparently the couple had had some understandable difficulty accepting the school diagnostician's new diagnosis of their child's learning disability.

Principal Matthews smiled at Paige, who thought she saw a hint of sadness in the older woman's eyes. "I'll stop by your office, Ms. Matthews," Paige said, and her boss squeezed her forearm gently before turning to talk with some of the other faculty.

Paige felt her stomach grumble and decided she'd finally been social enough; her appetite had returned with a vengeance. She navigated toward the barbecue spread and put together a plate of what was left at the buffet. Sitting down at an empty table, she suddenly remembered that she'd left her notes and favorite pen at the table she'd shared earlier with Liam. Just as she started to get up to fetch them, she felt someone standing behind her and looked over her shoulder to see Liam's large frame looming uncomfortably close. He smelled delicious—a unique mix of masculine soap and art supplies. "I'm sorry to bother you," he said, reaching down to hand her the pen and folder full of notes she'd just been thinking about, "but it looks like you forgot these." His hand brushed hers as he passed her belongings, and a confusing mix of desire and caution flowed through her.

"Thanks so much," she said, hoping he hadn't caught on to what she'd felt. "My grandmother gave me this pen when I got my first teaching job." The smile he'd worn so easily before was gone.

"And about Owen..." he said, before pausing, then continuing. "I've been thinking about him a lot and I know that there must be some way I can help him. It's a pretty big deal for a kid to lose the ability to speak to other kids his age. I'm just wondering, as his teacher, if there's anything more I should know."

Paige knew she was overreacting the minute she felt her heart begin to throb faster in her chest. Any of the desire she'd felt for Liam a moment ago vanished, to be replaced by maternal defensiveness. She knew he was just trying to help, but she was tired of people trying to tell her how to handle her son. Over the past six months she'd heard her fill of advice. She felt indignant when she thought that someone she'd just met, someone she'd have to interact with regularly, would offer her advice on her son's life.

She'd lost too many close friends already by being promoted to assistant principal. She'd also drifted apart from some that she and Mark had known as a couple, as well as friends who'd pushed too hard trying to tell her how Owen should be helped. They all had different opinions about what was best for him and seemed to forget that she was his mother and that she—and she alone—should know best. The comments and advice had slowly chipped away at the maternal instinct Paige had always trusted until she'd begun to wonder whether she was acting in Owen's best interests. And then there were the most hurtful comments, the ones from people who thought that she should just try forcing Owen to speak, as though he were withholding his words on purpose for attention. Attention? She wanted to scream at these people that attention seemed to be the last thing Owen wanted. In fact, he seemed, to her shattered heart, to want to withdraw from the world completely, to retreat from life at the ripe old age of six.

Like the thousands of similar overtures, Liam's offer to help felt as if it had been a criticism of her ability to parent masked as innocent concern.

"There's nothing more that you need to know," Paige snapped. "As I've said numerous times now, unless he has problems in class, I really don't want to talk about it any further."

Her answer didn't seem to satisfy him. She could see curiosity, but also kindness, behind his green eyes, neither of which she cared to indulge. She'd seen the same look countless times before.

"It's just that, the more I think about it, the more I'm certain I can help him," Liam insisted, taking a seat next to her as the cafeteria cleared.

Paige glanced at the clock. Almost time for her next parent meeting.

Why couldn't this man just leave her alone? What was it about her son that had him so intrigued? He'd said himself that he'd seen cases like Owen's before, so if her child wasn't unique, then why was he pushing so hard? Maybe she needed to be more direct because Liam apparently wasn't getting the message.

"Owen and I are fine, Mr. Campbell," she said abruptly, rising and gathering her still-full plate and notes. "Please just leave it alone."

She gave him no chance to respond and left the table, tossing her food into the trash on her way out the door.

Chapter Three

Liam could tell by Paige's reaction that he'd gone too far when he'd spoken to her at the meeting earlier that afternoon. Normally he wasn't so pushy, but there was just something about Owen that he couldn't resist. Although the boy hadn't spoken, Liam had seen a quiet seriousness, a depth and sweetness about him beyond his six years, an understanding and gentleness that the other kids seemed to pick up on. Rather than respond to Owen's silence by teasing or ignoring him, his peers seemed to stick by him.

Even though Owen probably continued to learn new vocabulary despite his lack of vocalization, he was missing out on getting to really connect with kids his age, on forming friendships that would carry him through high school and beyond. And if he were truthful with himself, Liam had to admit that Owen made him think of the children he'd like to have someday and reminded him of why he'd wanted kids in the first place. He knew he would have been incredibly proud to have a calm, sweet little guy like him to call his own.

And he knew in his heart of hearts that he could be a good father.

Liam pushed the thoughts from his mind as he cleaned up the evidence of another day in the art room. The mess around him was pretty tame and the kids were decent about helping him to clean up at the end of their class periods. But as the year went on, he knew the messes would grow larger and larger as the kids got braver with their projects. The thought made him smile.

He looked up from clearing a knee-level table to see Owen standing in the doorway, watching him work with large curious eyes. He hadn't had a chance to finish cleaning up his room before the teachers' meeting, so he'd returned to his classroom as soon as it let out. But he was surprised to see Owen there. Maybe the kid had waited for his mom in her office, gotten bored and wandered down to Liam's room.

"Hey, Owen," he said, hoping for, but not expecting, a response.

Owen shifted his small red backpack on his shoulders and stood nervously, as if waiting to be invited into the room.

"Come on in, buddy," Liam said, putting away the rest of the paints.

He glanced behind him as he took sticky brushes
to the sink in the corner and began to rinse them.
Owen had put his backpack in the cubby with his
name on it and had taken a seat at one of the tables.

"I have some brand-new clay in the cabinet over
there," Liam said. His hands still were wet, so he
pointed a shoulder to guide Owen in the right direction. "You're welcome to take it out and work with
it if you want."

Owen nodded and walked over to the cabinet.
After rummaging around for a moment, he found
the clay on the bottom shelf and chose a few colors
before bringing the soft sticks to the table where he'd
sat before. Liam was still worried that maybe the boy
had moseyed off from Paige's office, so he decided
to call her from the phone at his desk.

"Hey, Owen, I'm just going to let your mom know
that you're here, okay?" he said, picking up the re-
ceiver.

Owen nodded yes and Liam punched in Paige's
office extension.

"Hey, Emma. It's Liam Campbell," he said when
the receptionist picked up. "I was trying to reach Assistant Principal Graham. Is she in?"

Emma told Liam that Paige was in a meeting with
Principal Matthews, but that she would inform her
boss of Owen's whereabouts. He was still a little uncertain about having him there without her permis-
sion, but Emma hadn't seemed concerned and surely
Paige, cautious as she was, would know what her son
was up to. He planned to do the best he could to show
Paige that he knew what he was doing.

Liam joined Owen at the table and noticed he had chosen the red clay to work with. "Mind if I sit?" he asked.

Owen nodded that it was okay, so Liam perched on one of the kid-size chairs across from him. Liam took some of the clay and began shaping it into a car, enjoying the smooth, cool moisture of the blue material in his hands.

"I love working with clay," Liam said. "It feels really good to be able to build something with your own hands."

Owen said nothing and continued to shape the crimson dough with his small fingers, his tongue stuck out in deep concentration.

"And it's amazing," Liam continued, "that you can take a sort of weird and gross blob and make it into anything you want. Anything in the world."

Owen looked up at Liam then with wide eyes just a shade lighter than his mother's. Liam was struck by the thought that he'd love to see even the tiniest of smiles cross Owen's face again. He felt the same around the boy's mom.

It was amazing how the two of them tugged at his heartstrings after only a few days.

Amazing—and terrifying.

Liam continued to form the car he'd started while Owen shaped a dog with his red clay. Even though Owen didn't say a word, Liam's shoulders relaxed as he let the world go and worked to build something all his own.

* * *

When Paige left Principal Matthews's office late that afternoon, she felt simultaneously numb and fearful, as well as exhausted from the day's back-to-back meetings. Somehow she made it back to her own desk.

So, *she* was the first choice—the only choice, really, as she'd understood it—to take Ms. Matthews's place as principal.

On some level, she'd known she would at least be a candidate, but she'd assumed there would be a more qualified person to take the position. And though she would still have to interview and speak with the superintendent about her goals for the following year, Paige had gotten the impression that they would be mere formalities. Ms. Matthews had all but handed over her office to Paige during their meeting. It was an honor, and something she should be celebrating.

But, after her initial astonishment, a sense of apprehension spread through her.

How could she take on even more obligations and still offer Owen as much as he needed of her? How could she commit to more meetings, more intense conferences with parents and more supervisor duties than she already had and remain sane?

But then, how could she not?

The further she made it in her career, the more she could give to Owen: better therapy, a better home than their small condo and someday she hoped—if Owen's condition improved—finances that allowed for better college choices.

The weight of the impossible decision she had to make made her want to melt into her office chair, close the door and never leave. Sometimes, with tremendous guilt, she longed for the luxury of simply disappearing completely, just for a few moments. But she couldn't because Owen...

Oh, God... The breath rushed out of her lungs. *Where was Owen?*

Paige jumped up from her chair and threw open the door, rushing to Emma's desk.

Emma quickly pulled off her headset and looked at Paige as though her boss was crazy.

"Afternoon, Ms. Graham," Emma said, searching Paige's face for clues as to what might be going on. "Is something wrong?"

"It's Owen. I meant to call his babysitter earlier to see if she could pick him up and take him home today, but then I had the appointment with Principal Matthews and I forgot—and, oh, my God, how could I have forgotten—"

"Ms. Graham," Emma said, holding up a hand. "It's all right."

Paige could barely hear what Emma said as heat flared up through her chest and into her face.

"Mr. Campbell called an hour ago, just after you went in to speak to Principal Matthews. Owen's safe with him and everything seemed fine, so I didn't want to bother you during your meeting. And you went straight to your office and shut the door when you got back, so I figured you needed a little time to yourself. You looked so pale."

Paige rubbed her eyes and sat for a minute, holding her face in her hands.

"I can't believe I let this happen," she said to Emma.

"You're just stressed out," Emma said, sitting beside her. "Which is totally understandable. But there's nothing to worry about. Everything's okay."

"Don't bother with calling Mr. Campbell," Paige said. "I'll grab my things and go and get Owen myself. Thanks, Emma."

Paige went back for her purse, then closed up her office and said good-night to Emma on her way out. As she walked to Liam's classroom, she chastised herself again for being so irresponsible. Carelessness was something she disliked in others and she had always strived to keep it out of her own life.

The truth was, part of her *wanted to be principal*. She loved Peach Leaf Elementary, and she loved the faculty. Part of her had always yearned for the job, despite what her father had done all those years ago when he'd held the same position at Peach Leaf High School. She'd never admitted it to herself fully before, but there was a piece of her that thought that if she could become a principal, and do the job well, then somehow his abandonment of her mother and their family would be erased. She knew it was silly, but there it was all the same.

The hallways she walked now were the same she'd just left one afternoon, when everything changed. She was just Owen's age when her father had come home after work and told Paige's mother that he was seeing someone else, a teacher at the high school, and that he didn't love Paige's mom anymore. Paige had rushed out of her bedroom full of excitement to tell him about her day and had stopped on the stairwell when she heard the all-too-common yelling.

The words that had followed still roamed the back of her mind. He'd told her mother that he was going to build a new family—one that did not include his wife and daughters.

Paige had been Owen's age when her father had broken her heart, when her world had turned upside down, and he'd never come back, not even once, to see Paige or her sister, Emily.

The last she'd heard was that he'd moved to another town, where he'd taken a job as a principal at a high school far away from his unwanted family. But the damage was done. In their small town, the family name had been tarnished forever, at least in Paige's mind. She then worked hard to be the best student possible so that she could get enough scholarship money to send herself to college.

Despite everything that her father had done, she'd always wanted to teach, and he hadn't been able to take that away. So after finishing her master's degree, Paige had moved back home to take care of her mother when she'd gotten sick. She'd stayed, having met Mark and made a life with him.

In some ways, her father had become nothing but a distant memory, which most days she was able to block out completely.

But she remembered him now, as she struggled

against the doubt clouding her every thought. She'd forgotten to put Owen first today—she'd made a mistake—but she wasn't the same reckless parent her father had been. She couldn't bear the idea of Owen wondering where she'd been when she was supposed to have someone pick him up and take him home, couldn't bear the thought of Owen ever feeling abandoned as she had as a little girl.

Paige turned down a corridor and found the art room door open.

When she stepped in, the sight of Liam silently building what looked like a blue car with clay, and the look of pure delight on Owen's face as he shaped a red animal across the table, sucked the breath she'd just taken right back out of her.

She hadn't seen Owen smile that way, that freely, since before his father had died.

And, since then, she hadn't seen any man pay attention to her son with the obvious joy that Liam had all over his face. What she saw was something more than a teacher working with a student.

It was something special.

She stood for a moment, afraid to burst in and break the spell.

Just then, Liam caught her watching the two of them work. He smiled at her over Owen's head, and then turned back to her boy, without moving to put the clay away. The intensity of his smile at Owen made her pause. It was filled with the gentle tenderness she'd thought only a parent could feel for a child.

After putting on final touches, he stopped working on the blue car and held it up for Owen to see.

Owen stopped molding the red dog with his fingers and his eyes lit up at the car that Liam had shaped.

"Cool," said Owen, so softly that Paige wasn't sure she'd actually heard it.

But Liam looked up at her again and grinned, the corners crinkling around his forest-green eyes, and she knew she wasn't imagining anything.

Chapter Four

Liam pulled his eyes away from Paige and focused back on Owen, allowing her a moment of privacy to react to the fact that her son had spoken to someone other than her for the first time in a very, very long time. When he looked up again, Liam could see her eyes glistening with tears, which she quickly wiped away. She crossed her arms and stood watching, and Liam felt as though his heart was across the room with her. He always delighted in seeing his students or therapy-group kids succeed, but he felt now as if he were watching his own child cross a bridge that had seemed unsurpassable until that moment.

He tried not to let himself get too excited, though. It was common for kids like Owen to have a small breakthrough, and then digress into the shadows where they'd grown so comfortable hiding. Besides, even with this progress, it could take a few weeks for Owen to speak with regularity again.

He needed to communicate that to Paige. It was important for her to understand how delicate the next few days would be and how incredibly vital it was to Owen's further progression that she not make a big deal out of it. Owen needed to think everything was normal, to have the adults around him behave the way they had been for the past several weeks, so that he wouldn't feel their tension and retreat into silence.

But how hard it was to stay still when he wanted to sweep Paige into his arms and rejoice with her over this one moment of success.

After ensuring Owen was engaged with his clay, Liam rose from his seat and made his way toward Paige. She looked like she'd had one hell of a day. Her eyes were red with dark circles forming underneath, which, he was reluctant to admit, did nothing to detract from her natural beauty. As he neared her, he thought that nothing on earth could ever make her less lovely.

Dangerous thoughts indeed. He reminded himself that this was his boss he was thinking about.

"How has your day been?" he asked, hoping she would take his cue to just go with the relaxed conversation.

She looked at Liam curiously, and her eyes narrowed, clearly wondering if he had just witnessed the same thing that she had. He desperately wanted her to understand that he'd felt the significance of the moment as much as she had.

"It's been fine, I guess," she said, looking past Liam to stare at her son. "Did he just..."

"Yeah, he did, Ms. Graham, but..."

She had forgotten Liam and left him hanging on his words as she dropped her bag and took a step into the doorway.

"Ms. Graham," he said, reaching out and grabbing her arm.

She turned to look at him as if he'd slapped her, and he cursed himself for reacting so abruptly, especially when he was supposed to be the calm one here. He reminded himself that it wasn't *his* kid, after all, who'd just made a huge step in a positive direction.

Owen wasn't his child.

"What are you doing?" she said, glaring at him. "He just said a word. My son spoke, Mr. Campbell. Don't you realize that that's the first time he's said anything to anyone—*anyone*—besides me in six months?"

"Yes, Ms. Graham, I do understand that." She looked down at her arm, which he still held. He tried not to think about the way his whole hand fit around her small elbow or the softness of her creamy skin. How could he possibly be getting worked up over an *arm?* His boss's arm, no less.

But he had to make her understand before she unintentionally overwhelmed Owen.

"Ms. Graham, you have to understand something..."

"What—you mean other than the fact that he just took a monumental step toward getting better?"

Paige moved her arm out of his hand, and the next thing she did surprised the living daylights out of him.

"I understand that this is the most important thing that's happened to him—to me—in the past six months," she said, wrapping her arms around Liam in a tight hug before pulling back to grasp hold of both of his hands as she looked straight into his eyes.

Joy like nothing he'd ever seen shone out of those baby blues.

Her skin felt soft as satin in his hands as she held them with her own.

"And it's all because of you. I...we...have you to thank, Mr. Campbell," she said. The combination of her words and the way she was looking at him—as if he had her whole world balled up in the palm of his hand—caused uncomfortable, burning heat to fill his body.

He dropped her hands, quickly, and instantly regretted the harsh move when he saw a pink flush rise in the woman's cheeks as her eyes darted away from his. The last thing he wanted to do was embarrass her—or stop her from touching him. But he owed it to her to be honest. At that moment, he could either let her go on thinking everything would be okay from there on out, or he could tell her the truth and possibly break her heart.

Liam took a deep breath and decided to do the right thing, even though it might make him the bad guy to a woman who, much too quickly and very likely against her will, was climbing over his walls.

He looked down at his hands and then spoke, choosing his words with great care.

"Paige…you have to understand that what you do and say right now is important." Liam spoke softly in hopes that Owen wouldn't hear them. "He has to think that nothing weird happened. You have to make him understand that his saying something in front of me is normal, okay?" Liam glanced over at Owen before turning back to Paige.

He could tell she was trying to understand why she had to go against her feelings. Paige stared at her son and put a hand over her mouth, softly tapping her knuckles against her lips, as though assembling a million scattered thoughts into something coherent in her mind. After seconds passed that seemed like minutes, she forced her hands back to her sides and shoved them into her pockets.

"No, actually, I really don't understand. I really, really do not." This time she spoke softly and Liam could see that she truly did want to know what he was talking about. She seemed willing to at least consider following his lead. Maybe she was beginning to trust him, even after knowing him for only two days.

"Try to put yourself in Owen's shoes, okay?" Liam held his hands out, palms up, desperately wanting to show his sincerity and that he meant no harm. "You know that he's been quiet all this time because something has been bothering him deeply." Paige's eyes darkened and Liam scanned her face, looking for a sign. He knew he'd hit a nerve, but he had to keep going for Owen's sake, even if it bothered her.

"Something's been upsetting that kiddo to the point that he's felt like he can't speak to anyone but you. You're his safe place, you see. You have been all along," Liam said, and Paige's shoulders lowered slightly.

There. He was starting to have the effect he wanted.

"So now that he's said something, you—*we*—need to let him know that it's completely normal for him to speak. We don't want to freak him out so we have to just go with the flow."

Paige relaxed further, but her eyes were filled with what looked like confusion and pain as they met Liam's.

"Can I ask you something?" she said tentatively.

"Of course," he said. "Anything."

"I've just never understood, and the therapist has never really tried to explain it to me.... Why *this?*" Her forehead knit and she raised a palm in question.

"I'm afraid I don't understand what you mean." he said.

"Well, why this...this silence? Why has he chosen not to speak to anyone? Of all the ways he could react to what happened, why did he choose *this* way?"

Liam took a deep breath. He'd explained this so many times to parents who were doing the best they could for their children but still felt as if they hadn't done enough as they watched their children continue to struggle. "It's not that he's chosen this, Ms. Graham. It's just that, well, children don't, and can't, always rationalize the things they do or think through actions like us. They're brilliant people—don't get me wrong—it's just that they haven't learned to label everything the way we do. So if you were to ask Owen why he's not able to speak to anyone but you…"

"Which I've done," she said, rubbing her temples, her forehead creased. "Is that wrong?"

"No," Liam said. He wanted desperately to wrap his arms around her and tell her that he could tell she was a good parent and that what her son was going through wasn't her fault. "It's not wrong to ask. It's just that Owen may not have the language to answer that question or the ability to articulate clearly what's causing his body and mind to react the way they are."

Paige's eyebrows knit in concentration. Liam knew this was a lot for her to take, and he wondered why Owen's therapist hadn't made a better effort to help her understand. Perhaps she'd never felt comfortable enough to ask. No one could blame her for trusting a professional, and he'd bet Paige had hired the best doctor she could find. The psychologist had probably tried everything he could think of to help Owen.

But now the boy needed something different, and there was nothing wrong with that.

He vowed then and there to help Paige and Owen no matter what it cost or how much she resisted. He knew his therapy group would help Owen, but he had to find some way to get her on the same page.

"I guess I just thought all this time that at some point, somehow, it would just go away," Paige said, leaning against the doorway. "I thought that it was a phase."

She hesitated before continuing.

"After his father died, he was so quiet. I thought he just needed more time than the rest of us—Mark's family and me—to process it all. Mark's death was fairly traumatic—he was a firefighter and he was killed in a work-related incident. It was hard on me, for sure, but Owen lost a parent. I had no idea how he was feeling and it killed me that he wouldn't talk about it. And even though he still talks with me, he doesn't mention his father. It's like he's trying to erase what happened. He doesn't talk to Dr. Roberts or me about his dad—ever. And it took weeks after Mark died for Owen to start speaking to me again, so when he finally did, I just didn't push it. I let him lead the way."

The sadness in her eyes shook shards of glass out of a part of his broken heart he'd been certain he'd lost when Callie had left him—a part he wasn't sure he was ready to have opened and exposed again.

"We used to talk about everything, him and me. I miss my little boy. But sometimes a part of me just wants to tell him to snap out of it and stop all of this…craziness."

The second the word popped out of her mouth, a look of sorrowful guilt shrouded Paige's face.

She looked at Owen then, and Liam could see how the distance between the two of them hurt her. He dealt with this all the time, but it never got any easier to see that kind of pain between a parent and a child.

Yet, Owen had just taken a step, however small, toward getting better and being able to communicate again.

There was hope; that's what they needed to focus on now.

"I'll tell you what," Liam said, moving into Paige's line of vision to catch her attention. He took her forearms in his hands and held them there so he'd have her full concentration. "You, Assistant Principal Graham, need a break this weekend. And possibly a drink?" he asked, checking her eyes for a smile.

She grinned up at him and then closed her eyes, letting out a weary sigh she'd probably been holding in all day.

"I suppose you're right. A break, yes—a drink, maybe." They both laughed. Liam squeezed her arms a little before letting them go.

"I have an idea," he said. "You can say no if you like, but I want you to consider it before you answer."

"What is it?" she said warily, eyebrows raised in question. She was probably wondering if she could trust him.

"I've been staying at my sister's since I got to Peach Leaf. She's part of the reason I moved here."

Paige's eyes narrowed again.

"It's not anything bad, if that's what you're thinking," he said, smiling to reassure her. "I did pass the school's background check, you know." He winked at her.

She laughed a little.

"It's just that when I buy a house, I want it to be the right one. I plan on staying here a while," he said, trying not to think too much about her reaction to that. "So I've been staying with Rachel and her family until I find a permanent place to call home."

Paige nodded, but Liam could tell she was apprehensive about where this was going.

Just ask her. It's not a date. It. Is. Not. A. Date.

"Rachel and her husband have a great home and she's been bothering me because she thinks that since I've moved here I haven't met any...friends. If you agree to come over for lunch on Sunday, it'll get her off my back for at least a couple of days. You'd be doing me a big favor." He tilted his head toward her, urging her to offer a response.

Paige studied him and bit her lower lip. "I really don't know if that's such a good idea," she said.

"And the best part is that they have a swimming pool," he said, knowing that might seal it for Owen. "And Rachel has kids Owen's age—she homeschools them. I know he could probably use a little fun after today—and I know you could too," he said, checking her face for signs that she might agree.

He crossed his fingers, ignoring his sudden awareness of how much her answer meant beyond just helping Owen. He knew he was headed down a risky path, but as he waited for her to speak, watching her weigh his integrity with her sharp blue eyes, he knew that he no longer cared. All rationality aside, it was too late to backtrack now.

"It's just that I kind of am your boss," she said, "and I don't know how it will look if I go home with you."

Liam nodded, trying to hide his disappointment.

"It's not a date, Paige," he said, and the sound of her first name as it slid so easily past his lips sat heavily in the room between them. "And it's technically not my home."

"I guess it would be okay," she said finally. "And you're right, Owen would really enjoy it—he loves swimming."

Excitement rippled up Liam's spine, but he kept his expression neutral.

"Great, then. I'll email you the address," he said, sure she would refuse if he offered to pick her and Owen up.

"All right," she said with a tentative grin.

He knew her expression would carry him through the rest of the week.

I really need to get a grip, Paige thought to herself. For the rest of the week, she'd wavered a million times about whether or not she'd made the right decision in agreeing to have lunch with Liam. She told herself Owen needed the break, that he'd have a wonderful time playing in a swimming pool, especially with the temperatures still in the hundreds. She knew it would be good for her son to get to know some other kids his age outside of the friends he'd gone to school with his entire life, but, if she was completely honest, she knew she had another reason for going, too.

Despite her efforts, when she saw Liam in the hallways, it was getting hard to ignore the way she felt. The way her heart fluttered just a bit when she thought about those dark green eyes and how they fixated on her and held her in their grip. If he had been any other person outside of school, she might have considered the possibility of a new man in her life.

Wouldn't she?

When Mark had died, Paige had thought that part of her was over and done, that the rest of her life would be devoted completely to Owen. She'd never even considered the possibility of dating, let alone marrying again, and Liam shouldn't have brought all of that back.

But he had.

And now it was there in front of her—the heavy awareness of possibility between them—and she was losing focus from what should be her primary concerns, which were her son and her promotion.

Over the past few days, Paige had begun to feel her nerves objecting to it all. Her job now was challenging enough, and already she missed teaching, so was it a good idea to accept a more difficult position? But did she even have a choice?

"Hey, Paige, how've you been?"

Paige looked up from her turkey sandwich and saw Camille Henderson, Owen's main teacher, standing near the table with a pink cooler bag.

"Mind if I sit?"

"No, of course not," Paige said. "I'm glad for your company. How's the first week going for you?" She pulled out the chair next to her and moved her own lunch things so Cam could join her.

"Oh, you know how it goes. Jitters on the first day, chaos on the second and finally, near the end of the week, I'm getting names and personalities down. Now I'm starting to figure out who's going to try to give me a heart attack and who's going to remind me why I do this job in the first place." Cam's face lit up. She had been at Peach Leaf just a year longer than Paige, and they'd been classroom neighbors and had become good friends. Paige and the kids who were lucky to have Cam as their teacher could always count on her to bring a smile.

"Yeah, I know. I miss it sometimes," Paige said over her sandwich.

Cam's smile faded and her eyes grew serious.

"Listen, Paige," she said quietly. "I'm not sure if this is a good time, and I know you don't like to talk about Owen during school, which I completely understand...but I wanted to let you know something before I send out a note to all the parents." Paige felt her heart leap in her throat. She knew that she'd gotten a little overexcited the other day when Owen had spoken to Liam, and even thinking about it now made her feel a warm tenderness toward both her son and his art teacher. But Liam had been right when he'd warned her not to get too optimistic—her son still had much to work through—so the somber tone of Cam's voice set her on edge.

"Go on," she said.

Camille looked down at the food she'd unpacked from her cooler bag and seemed to avoid meeting Paige's eyes.

"I just wanted to let you know that we're having an…event…in a couple of weeks."

Paige wasn't sure she understood. Maybe Camille didn't have bad news about Owen after all. "What kind of event?" she asked, injecting cheer into her voice.

"It's a skit, Paige—for Parents' Night—and I want to give all the kids speaking parts."

Paige's stomach clenched, and suddenly she lost her appetite. "I see," she said. She didn't know what else to say. Cam meant no harm; she was a friend and a skilled instructor, and Paige understood why she would have all the students participate. Her son's delay was starting to affect him in ways that might be harmful. Most notably, he probably wouldn't be able to participate in this skit with his classmates and friends.

"It's important for the kids to do things like this at their age," Cam went on. "It's good for them to get in front of each other and their parents and perform. It helps them build their confidence and gets them used to memorization too."

Paige nodded. "I understand, and you're completely right, Cam. I just…"

Cam's expression softened and she reached out a

hand to cover Paige's. Paige resisted the urge to pull away. She knew that the concern she felt radiating from Cam came from a good place.

"You know this isn't about Owen," Cam said. "I'm not doing this to force him to do something he may not be ready for."

"I know. I just don't want to see him hurt in front of all those people, when he's the only one without a speaking part." She wasn't sure if she should tell Cam about what had happened with Liam. If she did, then Cam might assign her son a speaking role, expecting him to be all right, and the pressure might crush Owen's spirit and stamp out any chance of him progressing. However, she felt he deserved the chance to have the same experience as his classmates.

"I need to tell you something that happened recently, but it has to stay between us."

"I'm listening," Cam said.

"I'm sure you've met Li—Mr. Campbell, the new art teacher?"

"Um, yeah, I've met him." Camille blushed slightly and raised her eyebrows. "He's a complete hunk."

Paige tried to ignore the little flip of her stomach at Cam's reaction to Liam. Why should she care? Cam was single and a wonderful person, and could she really blame her friend for having a little crush on the new teacher?

"Well, anyway. The other day, I was late picking

up Owen and he ended up spending some time with Mr. Campbell."

Cam nodded.

"So when I went to the classroom to get Owen, I overheard him say something to the art teacher."

Camille's already large brown eyes widened and her mouth formed an "O."

"You're kidding!" She clasped her hands in front of her, and an enormous grin crossed her face.

"It wasn't anything much, really. He just said one word. And I'm not entirely sure if he was actually speaking to Mr. Campbell or if he was just talking to himself, but he definitely spoke in front of the teacher—in front of someone besides me."

"That's wonderful!" Cam said. "What did he say?"

Paige smiled. "He said 'cool.'"

Cam got up from the table and grabbed Paige in a bear hug before sitting down again. Paige pulled her sandwich closer and took a small bite. "It could mean nothing," she said. "Mr. Campbell said that I need to keep going on as though nothing amazing happened so that Owen doesn't get overwhelmed."

"That makes sense," Cam answered. "Sounds like the new art teacher is a pretty great guy."

"Yeah, he is."

Cam searched Paige's eyes.

"Am I detecting a trace of something a little more than an assistant principal and teacher relationship going on there?" Cam said, winking.

"No, of course not. It's nothing like that," she

lied. How she wished she could tell her friend the truth about her mixed-up, confusing emotions toward Liam, but doing so could put her new job offer in jeopardy. Paige knew what it would look like. If Liam ever got a promotion or was seen with Paige, questions would be raised, questions she couldn't afford to have swirling around if she wanted a life that was different from her father's and if she wanted a stable life for her son.

Cam looked up over her salad then, and Paige followed her line of vision to the doorway of the teacher's lounge.

And there he was.

Obviously feeling less shy than Paige herself, Liam strolled over to the table she shared with Cam.

"Hey, there," he said. Cam practically swooned, and Paige found herself irritated for some reason.

"Good afternoon, Mr. Campbell," Paige said, more formally and coldly than she had intended. She hoped the rest of the staff in the room couldn't see her blush. How ridiculous of her. They barely knew each other, and still she felt like a teenager with a stupid crush.

"Well, I've got to run, you two," said Cam. She got up and gathered the rest of her things. "Ms. Graham, I'll see you later and we can talk more about the skit."

Cam left the lunchroom just as the bell rang and the other teachers filed out to get their classes from the cafeteria. After a moment, the room was empty except for Paige and Liam.

"I see you're not eating much," he said, pointing

to Paige's discarded sandwich. "Don't mind if I do," he said, grabbing a grape. A smile played at the corners of his mouth, and Paige couldn't decide if she wanted to smack him or laugh. He had such a hold on her, and she hated it.

"I'm not hungry," she said.

"Is everything all right?" he asked.

He seemed completely at ease, despite the fact that they were the only two people there and were sharing a table. On the surface it probably looked like a lunch meeting, and if she had been with any other teacher, she wouldn't have given it a second thought. But to her, it felt like...like what, exactly? She was afraid to answer her own question.

"Yes, everything's fine," she lied. She seemed to be doing a lot of that lately.

"No, it isn't, Paige," Liam said, his grin soft and gentle. "I can see that something's wrong. Come on. Talk to me. I might be able to help."

"I don't need any help, thanks. Really, everything's fine."

"Yeah—that's your motto."

Liam's eyes darkened then, and Paige felt a sudden stab of guilt for shutting him out when he was only trying to help. She couldn't stand taking any more from him than he'd already given her when she had nothing to offer in return.

"All right, then," he said, his rich, warm voice turning her heart over in her chest and adding to her remorse. "Assistant Principal Graham doesn't need help from anybody."

She could hear the slight agitation growing in his voice. She realized she had hurt him this time, and the thought stung.

"I'm sorry," she said.

His eyes warmed, but they still held a hint of the injury her words had caused.

"We seem to be doing a lot of apologizing lately," he said, and Paige nodded. Would it really hurt if she decided to be honest with him for once?

"I found out today that Owen has a skit coming up for Parents' Night. Camille wants to give all the students in his class speaking parts, and, well, that's a problem for Owen. It's hard enough for him to speak in front of one person. So I can't even imagine how difficult it will be for him to get up in front of an entire audience of parents and his peers and say lines."

Liam listened quietly as she spoke. He seemed truly invested in every word she had to say. He was both kind and handsome, and he clearly loved children. Camille was right. He would be a catch for any available woman.

Too bad Paige was simply not one of them.

"May I say something?" Liam asked.

"Of course."

"I think this is good for the little guy. I know it will be challenging, but I think this will be a positive goal for him. It will give him a chance to be a part of something big. I think the last thing we would want is for him to be shut out, to be the only one up there without a speaking part."

"I agree. But there's so much more to it than

that. How in the world will he work up the nerve in front of all those people? What if he can't do it when the time comes? What if he's standing up there for his whole world to see and he freezes?" Paige felt her heart beating wildly as panic encroached. She touched a palm to her chest, and Liam reached across the table and set a hand on her upper arm. The warmth was deep and calming, and her nerves were soothed almost instantly.

"Hey, hey. It's okay." Paige let him hold her and, when she made no move to pull away, he touched her other arm too, and there they were, in the middle of the teacher's lounge, Liam holding on to her. It occurred to Paige that any of their colleagues could walk in at any time and see clearly what was going on. Somehow, though, the feeling of Liam's warm skin against hers outweighed the risk.

She wanted nothing more in that moment than for it to keep going. She thought if he pulled away, she would feel exposed and unsafe again. Alone. How had she gone from not needing anyone to needing *this* one?

"It's all right," he said, squeezing her hands in his own.

"I don't think so."

"It is—it will be." Liam removed his hands from hers and used one to push a strand of hair out of Paige's eyes.

"This is what we'll do. You'll come to my sister's like we talked about. I'll run by Camille's classroom this afternoon and ask her for the script they're going to use for the skit. When you and Owen come to lunch, we can look at it together and see what he thinks."

"Won't that be too much for him, though?"

"It might be—at first. But we need to keep the momentum going and show him that he's done well in talking to me.

"He needs to know he's on the right track. If we all look at the script together and praise him for getting a role in it like there's nothing weird about it, then he'll probably react positively. Plus, it will give him a heads-up before Camille tells the rest of the class about the skit, and Owen can decide whether or not he wants a speaking part. If he doesn't, we can tell Camille no, and she can assign him another part, without lines, without the rest of the class thinking anything of it, so he won't be embarrassed. If not, then we'll try something else."

The "we" in Liam's statement was clear. It sounded like he would be sticking around to see Owen through. Paige tried not to think too much about it. The last thing she needed was to get her hopes up, to put her faith in another man. Mark had been a loyal and loving husband and a great father, but he was gone—just like that. The same thing could happen to Liam if she put her heart out too far.

There was no way she could go through that again, and she knew Owen couldn't either. Nor would she put him in that position if she could help it.

But she knew Liam was right; they had to try, and for some reason, she trusted him.

And her trust had nothing to do with the way she was beginning to feel about him. *Absolutely nothing.*

"Okay, then we'll give it a try. For Owen."

"For Owen," Liam agreed.

"I have to go. I have an afternoon of meetings to get to and I need to look over my notes first," Paige said, collecting her things.

"See you Sunday, then?" She couldn't help but smile, and as she walked away, she knew he was watching her. She had to admit she didn't hate the idea.

Chapter Five

Liam was sifting through cantaloupes at Peach Leaf Produce on Main Street, Saturday afternoon, when he saw a familiar golden head of hair in his peripheral vision. He turned to make sure it was Paige before tossing a few pieces of the fruit alongside the rest into his basket and turning to follow. It was only after he'd reached the aisle she'd turned into that he thought twice about what he was doing. He was pretty sure she hadn't seen him—he could have just gotten on with his shopping and checked out without her noticing him. He hadn't even thought twice about saying hello, which unnerved him.

Yep. He was in pretty deep, all right. And it only got deeper each time he saw her.

Before he had time to ponder any further, she spotted him, and it was too late to do anything about it.

"Mr. Campbell," Paige said, turning from the shelves of wine in front of her. Her hair, he noticed with an inappropriate amount of gratification, was wild and windblown, and her cheeks, likely warm from the heat outside, were the exact shade of orange as the insides of the ripe local cantaloupes in his basket.

She was drop-dead gorgeous in a flowery tank top and fitted jeans that showed off the slender curves she hid at work. The light scent of her perfume—like a mix of summer rain and honeysuckle—made him want to step closer. His heart thumped so hard in his chest he was sure she could see its rhythm through his T-shirt.

"Please," he said, shifting his basket to one hand so he could reach out the other to shake hers. "Call me Liam. We're not at work." As he held her warm fingers in his own, he chided himself for the silly move. It was like he'd backtracked. Just yesterday, in the teacher's lounge, he'd held her and touched her face, and now he was back to square one, shaking hands with her like a stranger. Maybe it was for the best. Maybe he'd gone too far in being so open about his...his what? Concern? Care?

No. It was silly to pretend it wasn't much more than that. He was a grown man. And he would damn well act like one around this woman, even though she'd already all but stolen his heart after only a week of knowing him.

"Liam, then," she said, giving in. She shook his

hand before slowly letting go. He noticed that her fingers clung to his as they slipped away.

They stared at each other in uncomfortable silence for a moment before Paige astonished him by bursting out laughing. She covered her mouth self-consciously, but it was too late—her delight was contagious and he was already laughing with her.

"I'm sorry," she said, trying to catch her breath as the laughter subsided, her expression changing from joy to confusion to trepidation. "I don't know what's gotten into me. I'm no good at...at...this." She waved a hand at the air between them and then stopped abruptly.

It was as if her words had broken a dam, and all the things they were holding on to so tightly, all the things he knew they were both feeling but wouldn't dare say, came rushing over the top. He didn't want the sweet moment to pass, but he decided to take a risk.

He stepped closer to her, close enough to see that her blue eyes were rimmed with a deep gold, the same shade as her hair.

"And what is *this,* exactly?" he asked, waving his own hand as she had, holding her gaze despite the heat that threatened to burn his insides. He would make her face this—whatever it was—with him. They had both lost a lot before they'd even crossed paths, and it wasn't fair for him to go through this newness alone.

She started to turn away, but he caught her chin with his finger and turned her face toward his. It was the closest thing he had to forcing her to look at him. He knew that if he let her eyes slip away, the moment would pass. She would pretend it hadn't happened. And he couldn't allow her to do that.

"I asked you a question, Paige," he said, his tone walking a thin line between firm and gentle. "I'd really like it if you'd answer me."

She met his eyes. Hers were clouded with the fear and hesitance he expected, but something else was there, too, and he held on to it with all his might.

"I don't know," she said, biting her bottom lip as soon as she'd spoken.

Liam let go of her chin to run his forefinger down her cheek, slowly tracing her jawline all the way to her lips.

"Tell me something then, Paige. And be honest with me here."

She closed her eyes and nodded slowly.

"Do you want to find out?"

She didn't answer but only nodded again.

"Good. Because I do, too."

It was enough. For now. He leaned in slowly, giving her every chance to pull away, praying all the while she wouldn't. He brushed his lips softly against hers, then kissed her lightly, only once, the small motion causing every nerve in him to stand on edge.

He wanted so much more, but he would have to be satisfied with this for the time being. Paige needed her space. When she was ready, she would have to make the next move.

But, for the first time in a long time, he felt confident enough, and ready, to try again with a woman. *This* woman. The frayed edges Callie had left behind seemed to have softened just a bit since he'd met Paige.

Yet, if this was what she could do to him after just a few days, he was in real trouble.

When he pulled away from her, Paige's eyes remained closed, as if she might be afraid to open them and return to the real world, where they stood in a small grocery store, in a small town, where everyone could see them. He knew her enough now to know that fact would set her on edge.

She finally opened one eye, and then, seeing only him, the other eye.

He chuckled, and then her expression filled with wild irritation as the spell broke and she realized what had happened. She reached up a fist and socked him a good one right in the chest.

"Ouch," he said, moving back a step, amazed that such a tiny fist could hit so hard. "What on earth was that for?"

Paige glared at him and crossed her arms. "I should ask you the same thing," she answered, her cheeks turning bright pink.

"Did anyone ever tell you you're cute when you're angry, Ms. Graham?"

The comment earned him another punch, harder this time.

"The nerve you must have, kissing me like that in the middle of a grocery store when we've just met. What were you thinking?"

Now it was his turn to be annoyed. "I didn't exactly see you objecting, honey."

Paige rolled her eyes. "You kissed *me,* not the other way around," she said weakly, probably thinking the protest sounded as ridiculous as he did.

"You damn well didn't do much to stop me, now did you?"

Her eyes darted around at the truth in his words, and then she turned and focused on the shelves of wine, pretending to ignore him.

Liam picked his basket back up. So that's how it would be, then. Fair enough, he supposed...for the moment. He had to admit his move was sudden, and he'd been just as surprised by it as she had been. He'd give her some time to let it sink in, but he wasn't ready to let her out of his sight. The one taste of her had been plenty to make him hungry for more. He would do whatever he could to get her to spend the rest of the day with him, even if they had plans tomorrow.

She glanced over at him out of the corner of her eye. "Do you know anything about wine, Mr. Campbell?"

"Some," he said. "What is it you're looking for?"

"Actually," she said, still staring at the rows of bottles. "I was hoping to find something to bring to your sister's house for our lunch d—for our lunch... thing tomorrow." She tossed a smirk his way.

Touché. Hadn't it been he, after all, who had insisted it wasn't a date?

"I should tell you, Ms. Graham, that, although my sister would never let you know it, your gift would be most unwelcome."

Paige turned to face him and her mouth dropped open. "Excuse me?"

"It's just that, well, she's a few weeks pregnant. I'm afraid you'll have to find something else. Also, don't say anything about it—I'm the only one who knows. She's waiting to tell her husband when they go on vacation in a few weeks, so she can make it a surprise."

"Oh, my gosh. I had no idea," she said, covering her mouth. The motion caused her purse to slide down her shoulder and Liam reached out to adjust it, the simple act catching him by surprise. That was something he used to do for Callie all the time. He liked being able to do it now for someone whose small grateful smile let him know she really appreciated it. Sometimes it was those little things that he missed the most about having a woman to love.

"And how would you?" The rhetorical question visibly soothed Paige. "It's nothing at all. But...if you'd like...I can help you pick something different."

Paige's eyes crinkled around the corners. "I'd like that," she said. She glanced down at her watch. "I have a few hours before I have to pick up Owen from my sister's. You're sure you'd be willing to help out?"

"Of course," he answered, wisely keeping to himself the fact that he was getting to the point where he'd do just about anything for the confusing, self-contradicting, frustrating ball of fire called Paige.

Good Lord, that man could drive her crazy—infuriating her one minute and then arousing her the next with that perilously sexy smile of his.

Paige steadied herself as Liam led her away from the wine aisle, saving her from what would have been an incredibly embarrassing first impression. She was nervous enough as it was about meeting Liam's sister and all that the invitation did, or didn't, mean. The last thing she needed was to bring the wrong thing.

Liam was right—she really needed to relax. It had just been so long since she'd spent time around any new people. Her world was a constant cycle alternating between work, home and Owen that she'd lost touch with the importance of simply spending time around other people that weren't her colleagues. Although she'd been reluctant at first to accept Liam's invitation, the more she thought about it, the more she was beginning to look forward to hanging out with another mom.

But she would never admit any of that to the aggravating man who'd invited her. He was unbelievable. Kissing her in the middle of the grocery store on a Saturday, when any one of the school staff could walk right by and see them! If word got to Principal Matthews about the possibility of a relationship between Paige and a staff member, the new job would be off the table in a heartbeat. Rules were rules, and the Peach Leaf school system's rule against dating between faculty members was one she could probably thank her father for. And even though Paige hadn't made up her mind about whether or not she would accept it, she wasn't ready to give the prospect up quite yet. Not before she had time to give it serious thought.

She waited for Liam to purchase his groceries and walked with him outside to his truck, where he packed them into a small cooler full of ice to ward off the Texas heat. It was kind of him to offer to help her find a gift. Between the kindness of that and the kiss, her head was starting to spin. She could still feel the pressure of his mouth on hers, though it had lasted only an instant. It was one thing to see him across the hall at the school, where he might be able to light up her day with a single heart-stopping smile and those fiercely green eyes, but it was entirely another thing to have his body that near to her own. Having him so close had meant she wasn't able to hide the way her skin trembled at his touch.

Even if she'd been able to cover up her feelings before, there was no question now. She knew and he knew. And the longer she allowed it to go on, for moments like the one that had just happened to keep coming again and again each time they were in the same room, the harder it would be to back away.

And she knew that, eventually, she would have to back away.

She could kick herself for not being able to do so now. She wasn't the type to lead a man on, to make him think that there could be a future with her when she hadn't even figured out her own. She shouldn't allow him to do things for her as he had been. Things like helping her son get over the wall he'd built. How would she ever repay him? And how would she find the words to tell him that, as long as they both worked at the school, they could never truly be together? Despite all of that, here she was, unable to excuse herself and simply go home to relax alone until it was time to pick up Owen. Despite knowing that this could go nowhere, she was completely, totally, unable to say no when given the chance to spend time alone with Liam.

Oh, she was making such a mess. Paige tossed her head to clear her thoughts before they overwhelmed her. Maybe this was nothing. Maybe she was just something to occupy his time, and maybe he had no intentions beyond kissing her like a teenager and helping her pick out a gift for his sister.

The thought sounded ridiculous. She'd seen enough already to know Liam was a better man than that. He was serious about her and Owen. And the way that made her feel was enough to convince her to say yes to spending the afternoon with him.

"So, what do you have in mind?" she asked. "Seeing as how I've never met Rachel, I'm sure you know her better than I do."

Liam finished putting his produce in the cooler and closed his truck door before moving to her side. "Well, Rach is not complicated. You could bring her just about anything and she'd be happy as a clam."

"Anything but wine, that is."

Liam laughed a little. "Right, anything but wine. At least for the next eight months or so," he said.

Paige saw him reach out a hand and then choose instead to put it in his pocket. She was grateful. It would break her heart to refuse to hold hands with him, but she wasn't willing to deal with that yet.

Today, they would spend time together as friends. If anyone from work saw them, they would be doing nothing more than walking together, just as if she were out shopping with Cam.

Though she loved Peach Leaf, sometimes small-town life could be suffocating, as if she lived inside a bubble, where everyone breathed the same air, made the same assumptions and passed on the same gossip. That bubble had burst around her father, and everyone around him had suffered for it. She had no intention of putting Owen through the same kind of pain.

"I was thinking," he said, his words piercing through her thoughts, "that we could stop by the art gallery and take a look there. They have jewelry in the gift shop that I've seen her admire more than once when she thought no one was looking."

"Sounds great," Paige said, tossing him her warmest smile. The joy she felt around him was pure and simple, and she wished with all her might that she could sink into it without the fear that remained latched to her heart.

They walked the short distance to the small gallery, and Paige was thankful for the blast of cool air that greeted them inside. The building was beautiful and bright, with a skylight that let in all the sunshine without the accompanying heat. She had been there a few times before, including once at night for an event, and the stars had shone through then. It was incredibly romantic, actually—the kind of place she'd love to be in with Liam someday.

Someday. Maybe. There was no harm in dreaming, right?

Once inside, Liam glanced around, and then he did reach for her hand. Tentatively, she let him take it.

He led her around the gallery, telling her about each of the local artists responsible for the amazing creations on the walls. Though she'd seen them before, Paige had never experienced the paintings like she did now. Liam could see things in them that her eyes simply glossed over. To him, they were more than just colors on canvas—there was life in each piece. A bit of the artist lived there, right inside the tint and shading left behind by hundreds of brush-strokes.

She watched him as he spoke about the work, his eyes lit up with pure elation, and she could see why Owen had chosen to open up to the art teacher. He was a mature man, no doubt, but there was also the openness and lack of judgment she'd only ever witnessed in children. "Paige?"

It took a second for her to register Liam's voice over the din of her own thoughts. He squeezed her hand gently to get her attention.

"Hmm?" She met his eyes and saw amusement and tenderness in them.

"I asked if you're ready to go check out the gift shop yet," he said, chuckling at her momentary lapse into her own psyche.

"Sure. I'm ready," she said, taking a last look around the gallery, still amazed at how much she'd learned about its collection in such a short time.

Liam had a way of opening her eyes, of helping her to notice things that she would otherwise overlook. Maybe that was why Owen responded to him so well—perhaps he did the same for her child.

He led her to the small gift shop and helped her choose a pair of delicate, gorgeous turquoise earrings for Rachel. They cost no more than a decent bottle of wine, but Paige was pleased that her gift would be much more personal, though why it mattered so much, she wasn't willing to admit just yet. After, they bought a Coke and shared sips on the way back to their vehicles. When they arrived, Paige looked around quickly before clenching his T-shirt into her fists and pulling him toward her, the small paper bag of jewelry the only thing between them.

She kissed him gently at first, but only a few seconds passed before they were both breathless and hungry for something they knew they couldn't give in to, and she pulled away, despite every fiber of her being wanting to stay. Without saying another word, she walked to her car. Paige bet he was watching her leave, leaning against his pickup truck with his arms crossed, the afternoon sun casting shadows against the taut muscles his T-shirt did little to hide, and she knew she'd never again want anything as badly as she had in that moment.

Chapter Six

That Sunday, Liam pulled up to Rachel's house and admired the place for the hundredth time. More than a century old, it sat on a few acres near downtown Peach Leaf. The house and property had been a gift from their great-aunt, and it bore its long life with pride. On the land still sat the gazebo where his parents had been married all those years ago, a small vegetable garden, a pool and the guesthouse where he'd made his home for the past few months.

Even though he'd been too proud to take the main house for himself when his aunt had died, he would look for something similar when he was ready to start searching for his own home. He loved that Peach Leaf kept its history alive, and instead of sprawling new housing developments, there were antiques to educate and be admired.

Lately, though, he had begun to hope that maybe he wouldn't be alone when he started that search for a house. He thought of Paige and the way he'd kissed her the day before. He hadn't planned to do it, but it had come naturally and felt easy, as though he was meant to do it for the rest of his life. And then there was the totally unexpected kiss she'd given him...

Even though she'd resist it if he pushed her, he knew Paige was beginning to feel the same way toward him. He'd seen her eyes shade with something intense when he'd touched her; he hadn't missed the way she'd leaned ever so slightly into his hand. And she certainly hadn't pulled away when their lips had met. He knew he was getting too close, and if he kept at it, there wouldn't be a damn thing either of them could do except give in to their attraction. Doing so would change not just two lives, but three, and he wasn't sure either he or Paige was ready for that just yet.

Liam parked his truck out front and straightened his clothes as he walked to the door. He'd given up the comfort of his usual jeans and a soft T-shirt for khakis and a polo shirt. He knew Rachel would give him hell for it, but he wanted to show Paige that he was more than just a paint-covered art teacher.

"Hi, Uncle Liam!" his niece, Kaylie, said as she answered the door. Cake icing covered her face.

"Look at you," he said. "Did your brother attack you with the dessert?"

Kaylie laughed and Liam picked her up and set her on his shoulders to carry her into the kitchen, where he could smell his sister's delicious cooking. His stomach grumbled at the thought of a home-made lunch. Rachel invited him to join her family every night for dinner, and he knew she and her husband, Jackson, meant it when they said they loved his company, but Liam made a point not to interfere too much. As much as he adored their family, their joy was a painful reminder that he'd lost the chance to make his own.

Liam grabbed Rachel's shoulders from behind and wrapped her in a hug. She squealed and turned around to smack him gently on the arm, her smile giving her away.

"I see Kaylie's decorated you too," she said, and he noticed Rachel's face had spots of the same pink icing covering his niece's.

"What do you mean?" He did a once-over of his clothes to check for the sugary stuff.

"Should we tell him?" Rachel asked, lifting Kaylie down from his shoulders.

Kaylie giggled uncontrollably and pointed at his face.

"What?" he asked. Rachel joined in her daughter's laughter.

"Unless you're trying a new look and got into it with some dye," she said, "I'm pretty sure it's in your hair."

Great. All his efforts for Paige had been shot by an eight-year-old covered in pink goo.

"I'm going to the bathroom to see if I can't undo some of this damage. If Paige gets here before I'm back, don't scare her away." He stopped in the doorway and held out a warning finger; Rachel just rolled her eyes.

"Promise me."

"Okay, okay. I promise," she said, making sure he saw her crossing her fingers behind her back.

"I mean it. I know where you live."

He left the kitchen smiling to himself and was on his way to the powder room in the front hall when the doorbell chimed.

"Can you get that, sweetie?" Rachel called out to Liam. "My hands are covered in this stuff."

It was either clean up and leave Paige standing outside, waiting, or answer the door.

Liam ran a hand through his hair and hoped for the best as he pulled the door open.

"Well, hi there," he said. Paige and Owen stood outside on the porch. Liam noticed the nervous way she patted down her hair and fidgeted with her purse. He ignored the anxiety that crossed his mind, hoping she didn't have regrets about their time together the day before. He sure as hell didn't.

But then, he supposed he wasn't anyone to judge because it was very likely he had pink icing on top of his head at that very moment. He held only an inkling of optimism that Paige wouldn't notice.

"I hope I'm not too early."

"Not at all. You're in for a treat with Rachel's cooking. She's just pulling lunch out of the oven."

He smiled at her and stepped into the house and out of the way so she and Owen could come in.

He thought he'd escaped without Paige noticing, but then Owen reached up a hand and pointed directly at Liam's hair before turning to grin at his mother. Her eyes followed his arm and widened when they landed on his head. She covered her mouth.

"All right, what's so funny?"

Her eyes sparkled up at him, their blue clarity shining like sea glass in the sunlight that swept the foyer. Any uneasiness between them vanished, unlike the icing.

"I see you've been doing some baking yourself," she said and surprised him by poking a finger into his ribs. She turned to Owen as Liam jabbed at the goo. Instead of removing it, he succeeded only in spreading it further into his hair and all over his fingers. Now he would be forced to give in to Rachel's prodding and get that haircut sooner rather than later.

"So much for making a good…third…impression."

"The first wasn't as bad as you might think," Paige said before turning to her son. "And the second…well." She caught his eye over Owen's head as she tugged nervously on her child's shirt, adjusting his collar.

Liam felt a stupid grin cross his face. Paige smiled herself before looking away.

"Owen, how do you like Mr. Campbell's pink hair?"

The child looked between his mother and teacher, his smile melting Liam's heart yet again.

"I think it suits me just fine," Liam said and reached out to tousle Owen's hair—a motion that felt completely natural.

Strange, how all of his accomplishments paled in comparison to the not-so-small fact of this kid's smile. All of Liam's education and high honors, his teaching awards at the school he'd left—none of it mattered next to seeing Owen's face light up.

He knew he would feel the same way with his own child one day. But what would happen to Owen if he and Paige didn't end up together? His throat tightened as thoughts of the little guy's life passing by flooded Liam's mind before he could stop them.

He cupped a hand behind Paige's elbow and led his guests toward Rachel's kitchen.

As he walked beside her, he stole a glance.

Her hair, which he'd mostly seen in the somewhat severe ponytails she favored at school, and the messy but cute knot she'd worn it in the day before, hung loose around her shoulders, which were left bare by the soft pink tank she wore over a white cotton skirt. She brought to mind summer days by the sea, and he wished so hard that he could lean over, push her hair aside and kiss the space behind her ear. It would be soft and warm—inviting to his hungry lips. She would taste even sweeter than she had yesterday, he was certain.

Liam was thankful when Rachel called to him from the kitchen to hurry up and bring her guests on in so she could meet them. He'd have to be mighty careful to keep such enticing thoughts at bay. He reminded himself that he was here to help Owen, which he fully intended to do. And if he wasn't careful, Rachel's keen eye would see right past his shield and she would find out in no time what was going on inside his foolish head.

With that in mind, he released Paige's elbow to hold the French doors open and led them into the kitchen.

Rachel set a pan down on the granite island and removed oven mitts to shake Paige's outstretched hand, which she covered with both of hers. The two women smiled warmly at each other as Liam did the introductions.

"You didn't tell me Assistant Principal Graham was such a beauty," Rachel said, winking at Liam.

Wow. She was even quicker than he'd thought. Best just to keep his mouth shut. He had no intention of making Paige uncomfortable. There would be time another day to figure out where this thing between the two of them was headed, but not today. Today was about Owen.

Liam left them to get sweet tea from the refrigerator where Rachel always kept a pitcher in the summertime, and he could hear his two favorite women chatting easily at the dining room table where they'd settled. He checked on Owen and was pleased to see that he had joined Jeremy and Kaylie in the living room. Liam's seven- and eight-year-old nephew and niece were treating Owen as if he'd been their

friend forever. They didn't seem to even notice that
he was quiet.

Liam chuckled to himself. Owen probably couldn't
have gotten a word in for all their chatter even if he'd
wanted to. His niece and nephew were homeschooled
so they were always glad to meet new kids their age,
and their constant talk likely made Owen feel more
comfortable because it removed the pressure to talk.

Liam returned to the kitchen and found a tray in
one of Rachel's many cabinets, propped four glasses
and the pitcher on it—his brother-in-law, Jackson,
would be home soon—and joined the women in the
dining room.

"So he's a teacher and you're a principal and I'm
capable of connecting the dots, but how did you
two get to know each other so well?" Rachel asked,
passing out the glasses and filling them all with tea.
"Liam has talked nonstop about you since he started
at Peach Leaf."

Liam kicked Rachel gently under the table and she
shot him a look that was half venom and half sugar.
He made a mental note to get her for that one later.

Paige's skin turned a shade resembling the apples
resting in a bowl on the table, and she looked like
she might strangle Liam given half a chance, but she
recovered quickly. "We're just colleagues, actually.
Owen is in his art class." Paige took a sip of her tea
and her color returned to normal. "My son seems to
have taken to him," she said, her features relaxing.

"Well, he has that effect on people," his sister

said. "We certainly love him around here. Jeremy and Kaylie will be sad to see their uncle go."

Paige's face fell before she could cover it, and Liam's heart jumped.

"Are you going somewhere?" she asked. The concern in her features pleased him a lot more than it should have.

"She means when I move into my own place," he said, though he would have liked to ask her what difference it made if he was going somewhere. "I can't stay here forever."

"Actually, you could. No one else uses the guesthouse, and it suits you just fine, little brother." Rachel smiled over her tea glass, eyes filled with adoration for her sibling. "It's nice to have you in there." She turned to Paige. "We missed him when he lived in Abilene. It was too far for my taste." His sister winked at him across the table and raised the pitcher to refill their glasses.

He smiled back at Rachel. "You know I love the guesthouse and being close to you all, but I need a place of my own if I'm going to make a life in this town."

"Well, you've got me there. The guesthouse is way too small for a family," his sister said, and he was tempted to kick her in the shin again.

Geez. She wasn't even sneaky about it.

If Paige wasn't so sweet, surely she'd run out and not look back. Thankfully, Rachel changed the subject.

"So Owen's in Liam's class?"

"Yes," Paige said. "And he loves it. It's his favorite. He talks to me about it all the time."

"It has nothing to do with me really—it's the art. It gives him a way to express himself without having to speak."

Paige's eyes flew to her tea glass and Liam felt like a jerk for opening his big mouth about it before she had a chance to explain.

"Owen hasn't said much since his father died several months ago," Paige said softly. "He talks only to me. But recently, he was able to talk to Mr. Campbell. To Liam." Paige nodded at him across the table, and he caught her eye, holding it for a long moment.

"We're going to keep working on it and see if we can't get the guy reciting sonnets by the end of the year."

Rachel caught the glance between them and excused herself to fetch more tea. Liam excused himself from Paige and followed his sister into the kitchen.

As they left, he saw Paige smile. He knew her hopes were high, and he only wished he—and Owen—could live up to them.

"She's lovely," Rachel said. "And those earrings—be still my heart."

She put down the towel she'd been using to wipe the counter and turned to face him. Her eyes, exact replicas of his own, stared back at him, the cheer from a few moments before replaced with a seriousness he hadn't seen since he'd told her about his divorce.

"Honey, you know I love you with all my heart," she said. "But I need you to be straight with me here."

Liam braced himself for what was coming. Rachel had always been able to read him like a book—a fact that proved highly inconvenient when he didn't want to be studied.

"Are you sure you're helping her son and not yourself?"

"It's not like that, Rach," he lied. Her head tilted to the side and her eyes narrowed. He needed to work on keeping his feelings off his face.

She continued, not listening to him. "Not that I wouldn't love to see you with someone again." She crossed her arms over her chest. "You haven't been the same since that woman left you high and dry."

"Callie and I agreed on the divorce. We both had our reasons."

"Don't give me that, Liam. That woman broke your heart without reason and you know it. You deserve better, and I see how you look at this girl. It's good to see you happy again."

She was right, of course. If only it were that simple. Not so long ago, the mention of his ex-wife's name would have caused him pain and anger. Somehow, with Paige here enjoying herself with his family and her son playing with his niece and nephew, Callie's name stung with less intensity than ever before. He knew all too well the risk he was taking in bringing Paige, his boss, here. If he didn't keep a safe distance, he would end up in even more pain.

He also knew he was in too deep for it to matter. Liam had questions and doubts that had to be addressed, and soon. He needed to know if he was alone in his feelings. His instinct, not to mention that kiss she'd planted on him yesterday, told him that no, he wasn't the only one. But Paige was a hard shell to crack, and despite his feelings for her, he wasn't sure he was ready to get in that deep again if it would lead to the same end result. He needed to know where she stood. His heart had a different plan than his head, and there wasn't much he could do to stop it.

Rachel insisted she could finish getting lunch ready on her own, so Liam took two refilled glasses of tea into the living room, where he found Paige and the kids. He stood in the doorway, watching her as she wandered over to an end table filled with pictures.

"We all have bad hair days once in a while," he said, moving to stand next to her. He handed her a glass.

"I can't argue with that," she said, taking it. "But this one's pretty special." She took a sip and giggled at the photo of shaggy Liam when he'd been about Owen's age.

He rubbed his hair. It wasn't much shorter than it had been in the snapshot. "I've always hated getting my hair cut."

"I see that hasn't changed," she said and then surprised him once again. "It suits you." She lifted a hand and touched the pieces of his hair that brushed his shirt collar.

She was only inches away and Liam almost forgot that they were surrounded by half-pints. The sound of the kids laughing faded into the background, and for a few seconds, Paige held his eyes, her own wide-open and inviting in a way they hadn't been before now. He let her fingers linger there, so close to his neck that the tiny hairs stood up.

He liked having her there. Today, her soft pink tank allowed her femininity to show through, un-restrained. And without the trappings of her role as principal, without the sharp edges of her suits and heels, he could see only the woman in her—the woman who'd lost the man she'd loved, her child's father.

A wave of deep and strong emotion passed through him, much more intense than the previous day's physical attraction, and he knew that he would do anything to protect her from ever feeling anything so terrible again if she'd let him. In her company, he forgot everything but a deep desire to be the best man he could possibly be.

He couldn't help but wonder how his life might have turned out differently if Callie had been forth-coming early on about not wanting to have kids. Since the divorce, he'd often wondered if he'd per-manently missed out on the chance to be a father. Getting to be a dad would mean risking potential heartbreak again, wouldn't it?

Paige already had a kid—one that Liam was quickly growing fond of—and it didn't escape him that the three of them could be...a family.

But what if she wasn't ready to take that step? Perhaps he'd made a mistake inviting her here so soon without knowing how she truly felt. After all, they'd only really known each other for a week— in passing, no less. They had probably spent a total of five hours together, yet here he was, making the mistake of letting her in close—to a place in himself he'd barely begun to fix.

He took a step back from her, regretfully breaking the palpable sensuality of the moment. A sudden flash of unmistakable hurt crossed Paige's face.

He'd been selfish and shortsighted. The way she'd looked at him a moment ago, he knew she must have let her guard down, but maybe it was best if she raised it back up. For all of them.

"Uncle Liam! Uncle Liam!" Jeremy's shouts pulled his thoughts back and Paige turned away and cleared her throat.

Instantly, he regretted letting the moment pass. He might never get it back.

"Yes, Jeremy. What is it?" he asked.

"Mom says to make you guys come into the dining room. Lunch is ready."

"Well, we'd better get in there then, hadn't we?"

He picked up Kaylie and put her on his shoulders again, causing her to squeal. He reached down to grab Owen's outstretched hand. The small warmth of it spread throughout his bones and reached into his heart.

If he pushed Paige away and didn't give her the chance to decide for herself, then he wouldn't just lose her. He would lose Owen, too, and he was already falling for both of them. But he didn't want in on something without her being fully on the same page. She didn't deserve that, either. They'd both been hurt too much and needed the real thing this time around.

The five of them filed into the kitchen. Jackson had come in through the garage door and was kissing his wife's cheek when they got to the dining room.

"Hey, guys," he said.

"Dad!" Jeremy ran to hug him and Kaylie began banging Liam's shoulders to put her down, which he did.

Jackson hugged his kids, then Liam, who introduced his brother-in-law to Paige and Owen as they sat down to lunch. Paige insisted on helping Rachel, who promptly refused and served them all before sitting down herself to a mouthwatering meal.

When they finished, Liam changed into swim trunks while Paige helped Rachel clear the table, and finally they joined Liam, Jackson and the kids outside on the patio. Liam saw her take Owen into the pool house and he came out dressed for the water.

"Okay, sweetheart. Go on in with Jeremy and Kaylie. I'll be right here when you're ready to get out. And you can call me if you need me."

"Okay, Mom," Owen said, in front of all of them.

Paige raised a hand to her mouth, but luckily Owen was on his way to jump into the pool so he didn't catch the emotion on her face. She looked at Liam, who gave her a thumbs-up across the water before she turned away to wipe what he suspected was a tear from her eye.

Liam's heart swelled with a new kind of pride. He'd experienced success like this before, but somehow this was different. This time, he was fairly certain, it had something to do with love.

Chapter Seven

Paige almost pinched herself; the day was going so well. Liam's family was fantastic and Owen seemed to be having a great time. The afternoon flew by as she watched Liam swim with the kids. She could tell he genuinely loved them, and Liam seamlessly integrated Owen in with Jeremy and Kaylie, as if her son was a natural part of their family.

She'd had to stop herself from daydreaming several times throughout the afternoon. She'd gotten lost in the sounds of splashing and happy shrieks as she lounged on the deck and read only a few pages of the script Cam had given her to look over. Cam had assigned Owen one of the smaller roles. He would have a few words early on so that he could get them out of the way and then enjoy the rest of the skit knowing he'd—fingers crossed—succeeded in delivering them.

Paige was surprised with the speed at which Owen seemed to be progressing after that tiny but powerful word he'd spoken to Liam. Since they had been at Rachel's, she'd overheard Owen say a couple of words to Jeremy. He was a little shy with Kaylie, but Paige chalked that up to her being a girl and having "cooties," as her students always used to say.

As happy as she felt, though, she couldn't help the pang of guilt that slipped in alongside her joy. How could she have spent all this time trying to make sure that her son had all the best resources available to him—resources she'd made many sacrifices for, as any mother would—without Owen getting any better? Then, in walked Liam, and after a single week of art class with him, Owen had said more to other people than in the past six months combined? Granted, compared to most kids his age, he still had a long way to go before his social skills were back to normal, but she knew better than to compare her child to other children too often.

Owen was doing great—by Owen's standards. For now, that was all that mattered. They would concentrate on one step at a time; they would walk together until Owen could run alongside his peers again. A few words to Jeremy was enough today. Tomorrow, they would face that day's challenges, and she would let Owen set the pace.

Her doubts lessened a little and she turned her attention back to the pages in her lap. Paige had checked with Cam to see which part Owen would play, and she'd given a copy of the script to Liam, who had promised to pass it along to Rachel to give to her crew so they could rehearse with him. Liam had assured Paige that Jeremy and Kaylie were mature for their ages, enough to handle Owen's feelings carefully and sensitively. Still, her heart raced, with equal parts anticipation and fear. She had her doubts that Owen would want to practice the skit in front of anyone, and she would be devastated if he caught on to the fact that the whole day had been basically orchestrated for his benefit. But she was willing to try anything to help him, and, against her initial judgment, she'd begun to trust Liam's methods.

She'd begun to trust him, period—a thought she didn't care to examine too closely any time soon. No matter how great he was with her son, or how often he made her laugh in spite of herself, or how incredible he looked sloshing around the pool in his swim trunks, the full masculine beauty of his toned body on display…none of that mattered. She simply could not get involved with faculty. It would mean the loss of the principal job for certain.

And shouldn't she still miss Mark? The sharp stabbing pain she'd felt in the weeks following his death—weeks when Owen had stayed with her sister, Emily, because Paige couldn't seem to manage to pull herself out of bed those mornings—had long passed. But the fact remained that she'd built a life with her husband—a life that she'd then lost in the span of a few moments.

Did she have it in her to start over with someone new, to do it all over again? It couldn't be with Liam, she knew in the back of her mind, but could she do that with anyone? The problem was, she could imagine all of it with Liam and no one else. That's what scared her the most, the way she could easily lose herself in him if she wasn't careful. Just like earlier, when she'd carelessly touched his hair without giving it a single thought. Just like yesterday, when she'd stupidly kissed the living daylights out of him in the middle of town.

It was one thing to let Liam help Owen. It was quite another to become involved with him herself. And what would he be for her? A warm body? A place to let go? A distraction from her guilt of not missing Mark enough? The answer was that he would more likely be a distraction from being the best mom she could to a child who needed her—a distraction she couldn't afford.

Later, when Liam, Jackson and the kids had rinsed away the chlorine and dried off, they all settled in the living room and Paige helped Rachel get snacks together. Liam's sister was incredibly easy to be around; she was the perfect mix of nonchalance and open honesty. She made Paige feel as if the two of them had been friends forever, another reminder that she was sinking deeper and deeper into something she would have a hell of a time digging her way out of.

As soon as the year was over, and Owen passed the art class, not only would they lose Liam, but she would have no reason to see Rachel or her family again—a thought that was rapidly becoming too unpleasant to bear. Not to mention Owen's instant bond with Jeremy. He'd even had the courage to splash Kaylie a couple of times in the pool when he'd thought no one was looking.

"Okay," Rachel said, pulling the last kernels of popcorn out of an old-fashioned pan. "I think we're good here." She set two massive bowls on the counter.

Paige pulled melted butter out of the microwave. "It looks delicious. I'm sure the kids will love it after burning off all that energy."

"Are you kidding?" Rachel said. "One of these bowls is for us."

Paige giggled.

"If we're lucky, they'll crash later and give us grown-ups some peace and quiet."

Paige agreed. "Owen will just be glad he's getting popcorn that's not from a bag. I don't have too much time to make home-cooked food anymore with my job. When it comes to choosing between cooking and spending time with him, I'll always choose the time." As the words came out, Paige felt her face heat. "You must think I'm terrible."

Rachel set down the bowl she'd filled and wiped her hands on a towel. She faced Paige. "Now, sweetie, why in the world would I think something like that?"

Again, she'd said too much without thinking. "It's just that...well, it must be really nice to get to stay home with your kids while they're young." Paige caught herself just before she mentioned the secret new baby Liam had told her about. She traced a finger along the countertop. "I always wanted more kids. When Owen was young and I was teaching, I had time for everything, since my kindergarten class got out early afternoon. As much as I enjoyed it, I planned to leave teaching when we had another baby. But when Mark was killed...well, I needed the job, of course." She left unsaid her sadness at the thought of never having any more kids.

Rachel's eyes were intense and sympathetic as she listened, but there was no trace of the pity Paige was used to seeing when she talked about the difficult past. What she saw instead looked more like admiration. "And when they offered you the job of assistant principal," she said, "you had to take it."

"Exactly. And I really like it a lot of the time." She picked up a few pieces of popcorn and tossed them into her mouth.

Rachel did the same.

"But I miss Owen. I feel like time is slipping by so fast and I'm missing it."

"I really shouldn't say this, but Liam told me a little bit about Owen. And I just want to tell you that it's not your fault—what's going on with your little guy."

At the words from another mom, Paige felt unexpected tears threaten from behind her eyes. She'd heard the same phrase from Owen's therapist probably more than a hundred times, but never had they delivered such impact as they did coming from this kind near-stranger.

"I mean it. I know we only just met, but your love for your son is plain as day," Rachel went on.

Paige was thankful she didn't have to speak. She wasn't sure she could have.

"And I can see that he's a special kid. But there's something else you should know, honey."

Paige braced herself, expecting a sad story of warning about a kid that Jeremy or Kaylie had known who'd struggled like Owen. What she heard instead rattled her to her core.

"It's not just Owen that brought you here."

Rachel laughed at what must have been a look of horror on Paige's face.

"Don't give me that look. Surely you know that my little brother's got it bad for you. Oh, yeah. He tries not to, but he can't help but slip your name into conversations about everything you could think of. For the past week, your name has popped up surrounding anything from what to have for dinner to… flower pots, of all things."

Paige laughed. "I'm sorry—flower pots?"

"Yes. Flower pots. I took the man shopping with me to the garden store this morning and we came across a blue planter that was—I quote—'the exact color of Paige's eyes.' I don't think I was meant to hear it since it was a whisper, but I did. Maybe it's the artist in him, just noticing things like that, but I didn't get that impression."

Paige rolled her eyes at Rachel's joking.

"What? Don't believe me? The darn thing's sitting

right outside on the deck as we speak. You passed it on your way in from the pool."

Paige's response caught in her throat before it could fully form into coherent words. She swallowed. "I don't know what to say."

Rachel waved a hand at her. "It's okay. You don't have to say anything at all." Her features straightened into serious lines. "But—if I may?"

"Of course," Paige said.

"I've seen the way he dotes on you," Rachel continued. "And although I'm glad to see him back from where Callie left him, I worry about that man. He hasn't put himself out there like this since her."

Paige knew a thinly veiled "don't break his heart" warning when she heard one, and she didn't blame Rachel. Liam was clearly special—a fact she could no longer escape—and, if their roles were reversed, she would want to protect him too.

"He'd kill me, of course, if he knew I'd said anything. This is just between you and me. But he's not the only one who's taken to you."

Rachel smiled and softly tapped a finger to Paige's forearm. "We've all enjoyed having you today, and you're welcome here any time. Sometimes you come across a person who just...fits."

A tear slipped past its barricade and slid down Paige's cheek, and she made no move to wipe it away. Amazingly, in one day, she'd met people who felt as much like family as her own.

She felt like she'd come home.

A burst of laughter interrupted her thoughts as it

echoed through the house. Paige and Rachel made their way to the living room to join Liam, Jackson and the kids. Paige had no idea how he'd done it, but Liam had the lot of them reading Owen's class skit out loud. Props were scattered all over the oak floor. Owen was shrouded in a blue cape covered in yellow stars, a smile stretched wide across his face. Liam was decked out in a bowler hat, tweed jacket and fake mustache that hadn't quite been adhered properly and dangled halfway into his mouth as he rehearsed lines. Jeremy and Kaylie had on equally silly, mismatched costumes. A loud laugh escaped Paige at the ridiculous scene in front of her.

"Goodness," Rachel said, coming up behind her with the popcorn. "What in the world have we walked into?"

"I was wondering the very same thing."

"We're acting, Mom!" Owen shouted above the noise in the living room, nearly knocking Paige completely off her feet. She and her son shared a look across the room, and then Owen went on playing with the others as if a small miracle had not occurred.

On their way home later, Paige watched Liam's face from the corner of her eye as he drove. She and Owen had stayed through dinner—Liam's family had ordered pizza and refused to allow Paige to pay for it. Liam had offered to take the two of them home, despite the fact that her condo was only a few minutes' walk from Rachel's. He said he didn't want them walking in the dark.

Rachel and Paige had shared a laugh at that because Peach Leaf was about the safest place in the world. The most interesting thing likely to happen if she and her son had walked would have been that someone would have stopped to give them a ride, but she was grateful all the same. It was just another kindness he'd done that made her like him more and more each minute. Aside from being a fantastic teacher, and seemingly an asset to her son getting well, he was also old-fashioned in the best way—a gentleman. She was in deep trouble.

"Just around the corner up there," she said, directing Liam to their condo. The drive had taken less than five minutes. He pulled in and Paige opened her door before he could come around and let her out. She needed to keep some distance.

As the day had gone on, they had shared more than a few knowing glances, and Liam had made it fairly clear that his spending time with her wasn't only because of Owen. She felt flattered, touched and definitely attracted to him, but the fear she felt at what might happen if someone at school found out…if they began to date…or even looked like they were dating…

She had to think about her job. And she needed to prove that she was the right choice to take Principal Matthews's place. Any wrong move with the gorgeous man next to her and she could lose everything. Surely he knew that. And surely he would be concerned for his own job, too. Art teacher positions weren't in mass quantity, especially in a town with only one elementary school.

So why, then, did it still feel so incredible when he looked at her? He could undo her with just a glance from those amazing deep green eyes. He made her feel an attraction she hadn't in a long time, and his looks were just extra. She enjoyed every moment with him; he was funny, intelligent and masculine but also softhearted.

And the way he was with Owen...she hadn't seen her child take to anyone like he had to Liam. She knew Owen missed his father, but being with Liam seemed to make it less painful for him. And she liked seeing him do things with a man again.

The truth was, Liam filled a spot in Owen's life she knew she couldn't. It hurt her a little to admit, but she knew, at the bottom of her heart, that she could never make up for the loss of his father. She could be a wonderful parent on her own, but she wanted Owen to have experiences with a father figure. She had to face the possibility that things might be better with this man around.

"Here we are," Liam whispered. Paige looked over her shoulder and noticed Owen was completely asleep in the backseat. She laughed quietly.

"He's exhausted, the poor guy."

"He's just had a big day, is all," Liam said. Paige looked down at her hands, making no motion to unfasten her seatbelt. She knew as soon as she did that the day would be over, and she didn't want the spell broken just yet. Part of her—a stronger part than she was ready for—wanted Liam to turn around and drive her to his guesthouse. To take her in and give her what she'd been without since Mark's death.

But what about Owen?

She pushed the button to unbuckle her seatbelt and reached for the door handle. Liam caught her arm next to him and pulled her gently closer. He leaned in slowly, and Paige did nothing to stop him. It was as though her heart refused to take direction from her head.

"Mom," Owen said suddenly from the backseat, his voice groggy from sleep. She pulled away and Liam smiled softly before settling back against his seat.

"Yes, sweetie?" She nervously wiped her hair from her face and turned toward her son.

"Can Mr. Campbell and I have a sleepover?"

Paige was thankful for the darkness surrounding them in the cab of Liam's truck. She knew her embarrassment would have otherwise been unmistakable. Liam, however, simply laughed softly.

"I'd better get on home, big guy," he said, turning to face Owen. "But I'll see you again tomorrow at school. How does that sound?"

"Okay," said Owen, looking straight at Liam. He didn't even seem shy about it, and Paige felt as though she would melt into the leather seat.

"Let's get you two inside," Liam said, opening his door. He walked over to Paige's side and helped her out. She started toward the cab's back door, but Liam held out a hand for her to stay still. He opened

Owen's door and, as though he had done it a million times before, unbuckled her son and lifted him out of the seat in a fluid motion, just like Owen's father had always done.

Paige forced herself to move and pulled out her keys to open her front door. She held it open for Liam and once inside, pointed the way to Owen's room. Liam carried the child upstairs and laid him across his race-car-shaped bed. Paige pulled off Owen's shoes and clothes and pulled the covers over him before kissing his smooth, warm forehead. "Good night, my love," she whispered.

She turned to see Liam standing outside the doorway. He was watching them from the hallway where he'd moved, probably to give her a private moment with her son. She wasn't sure if her heart would soar or break as she walked toward him. His eyes appeared almost black in the small ray of light seeping through from the hall. Her mouth was suddenly dry and her heart began to beat so fast she could barely think of what to do next.

"Paige..." Liam said. A rush of air left her lips and she realized she'd been holding her breath.

"Thanks so much for...for this," she said, gesturing toward Owen's room.

"It's my pleasure," he said. It would all be fine from here as long as Liam just walked down the stairs and back out to his truck. She felt far more out of control than she was used to, and it bothered her. There he was, looking amazing in the darkness...and after the kisses they'd shared yesterday, she knew that more would be...it would be too much.

He walked toward her, closing the gap between them in just a few steps, until he was close...far too close.

"Paige," he continued. "I just want to tell you that I had a wonderful time with you today. I'm glad you came."

She fought to form coherent words from a brain that failed her completely at the moment.

"I am, too," she finally choked out. Her voice sounded embarrassingly squeaky and she suddenly felt like a teenager instead of the almost-principal at the only elementary school in town. She should have more control than that.

Maybe if she just approached the situation as she would a parent with a child at her school. Surely that would help her regain her footing. She'd lost it so badly yesterday when she'd kissed him, she knew she couldn't handle it if it happened again, or if something more happened today.

"I think it's probably best if you go home now," she said, stepping slightly away from warm, spicy scent of his skin. Instead of making his way down the stairs as she'd half hoped he would, Liam only stepped closer, until he was touching her again. She could feel his warm, firm chest against her own; his arms wrapped around her lower back, and when she dared to look up, she saw his mouth only an inch away from her forehead.

"Paige," he said, his voice so low and throaty. "I

said I had a wonderful time today and yesterday. I meant it, and I'm not ready for it to be over. I know you're not either, so stop fighting it so damn hard."

She wanted him to come closer still as much as she wanted him as far away as possible. Why couldn't she make up her mind? Why couldn't she just tell him to go again before they made a mistake that couldn't be undone?

And then he did exactly what she'd hoped he wouldn't.

He reached down and pressed his warm lips against hers, softly at first, and then, when she didn't protest, more firmly. Paige's heart leapt. Kissing him felt as monumental as it had the day before, if not more so. At the same time, it seemed comfortable, as though they'd always meant to do it.

Liam wrapped his arms tighter around her and then reached a hand up to pull her head nearer to his, enveloping her and deepening the kiss. She felt her legs go weak beneath her, as his hands slid underneath her blouse and up the sides of her abdomen, sending blinding electricity through her body. He pulled her closer still as his fingers caressed her lower back.

It was too late. Even if she'd wanted to, there was nothing she could do to stop what was happening, and she wasn't even sure anymore that she wanted it to stop. She'd forgotten what it was like to have a man touch her that way, and she wanted desperately to remember.

So when he lifted her in his arms as though she

weighed nothing, she let him. And when he asked her with his eyes where her bedroom was, she silently lifted a finger to point the way.

And, after he'd shown her how amazing it was to be wanted again by an incredible man, when he took her heart for his own...there wasn't a thing in the world she could do to stop him.

Chapter Eight

After a month of dating Paige, Liam was discovering that nothing was ever a simple yes or no. She was as stubborn as the day he'd met her, and for some reason, it was one of the things he was beginning to love most about her.

She challenged him at every turn, but she was worth every obstacle she built around herself. Each new thing he found out about her just fueled his hunger for more. It would take a lifetime to get to know her completely, and he was beginning to think he might be willing to give it that much time.

"So, where to first?" he asked as he fastened his seatbelt in Paige's passenger seat.

She grinned. Even though he'd spent hours with her and Owen, mostly working on the boy's speech, which continued to improve, she'd only recently agreed to their first *real* date. She would allow him to take her to dinner, but only if he promised not to kiss her again in public, and only under the guise that she was showing him around town as a friendly favor, nothing more. He'd played along and teased her as though he minded, but of course he didn't. He'd let Paige Graham show him around a blank white room if it meant he could spend time with her.

"It's a secret," she said, pulling a handkerchief out of her purse and passing it to him across the truck's cab seat. "Put this on."

"Well, Ms. Graham. I had no idea you were going to blindfold me or I would have suggested we skip dinner."

Paige punched him lightly in the shoulder and laughed at him. The sound of it was contagious and he laughed, too.

"Not quite," she said. "You'll see. I think you'll like it. The place I'm taking you has history, culture and art all in one."

"In this tiny town?"

"Hey, mister. This town is a wonderful place, which you'll see in time." Her voice trailed upward on her last words and Liam heard the question in it.

"I can see that already," he said, looking into her blue eyes. He was constantly amazed at their changing shades. When he'd been working toward his art-therapy certification, he'd spent hours and hours learning how many incredible hues there could be of one basic color. Blue was never simply blue—it was an endless palette of possibility—and Paige's eyes seemed to hold all of them at one time.

He'd seen Paris as an undergrad and had studied at some of the finest museums for his master's degree, but sitting there, in the seconds before she covered his own eyes and obscured the view, he had the feeling he could stare forever at her and be satisfied for a lifetime.

"Okay. Now, can you see anything?"

"Just the light from underneath. Nothing more. Unfortunately." He thought he could feel her smile next to him and wished he could sneak a glance.

"It's only temporary. I just don't want you making fun of me before we get there."

"Now I'm really concerned. You're not taking me to see the world's largest turnip or something, are you?" The truth was, he was falling in love with Peach Leaf and didn't miss traveling nearly as much he had when he'd first gotten there. The itch to go had dissolved from him almost as soon as he'd arrived.

He just enjoyed teasing Paige, enjoyed the way she turned from assistant principal into the most exciting and fun woman he'd ever had the pleasure of spending time with. He wondered if she knew she was different outside of her job, if she really loved what she did, even though it seemed to cause her stress more than anything. She'd opened up to him over the past weeks about how hard she'd worked to snag her current job and how much harder still it would be to be the main principal when Matthews left. But he knew she did everything for Owen, and he supposed he would have done the same if he had a child.

They drove for what seemed like ten minutes or so and finally Liam felt Paige's truck pull to a stop.

"Here we are," she said. He heard her engage the parking break.

"Am I free now?"

"All right. Go ahead and take off your blindfold."

Liam reached up and pulled the bandanna from his eyes. The first thing he saw was a large white clapboard building that looked like an old library. The sign above it read "Peach Leaf Pioneer Museum." She was never predictable, that was for sure. Childlike delight bubbled up at the thought of an afternoon there with her, but his initial feeling was joined almost immediately by something darker.

"Well?" she asked.

Liam looked over at her and his heart did a little turn at the expression on her face. She clearly loved this place and wanted him to feel the same way, but he couldn't let her see that he knew why she'd chosen this spot. Their visit could easily be traced to purely professional and educational reasons should they have the misfortune to happen upon any fellow employees.

Clever Paige.

"It's fantastic," he said, reaching out to touch a finger to her chin. He was rewarded with one of her beautiful smiles that warmed him even more than the Texas sun seeping through the car window, almost enough to burn away the dull ache in his heart.

"You mean it?"

"Of course," he said truthfully. "I loved going to these kinds of places as a kid."

Happy relief washed over her face.

"Well, Mr. Campbell. Let's go inside."

Liam got out of the car first and walked around to Paige's side to open her door—something she'd finally decided to allow him to do regularly. She'd resisted the first several times they'd gone anywhere together, but she had obviously realized that she deserved to be treated like the lady she was, or at least she let him think so. Now she didn't race him to make sure she was first to every door they came across.

They walked inside and grabbed a map of all of the buildings on the grounds. First they visited an old blacksmith shop, and a docent helped the two of them make a horseshoe to give Owen. Liam couldn't stop thinking about how adorable Paige had looked in that helmet, its size engulfing her pretty head, and the cute way she squinted in concentration as she'd formed the molten metal.

Afterward they shared a biscuit made by hand at what was once a baker's shop. The baked dough had been flaky and soft, leaving crumbs around Paige's full lips, which she'd let him brush away with his fingers. He would have liked much better to have kissed them off, but any opportunity to touch her was a chance he wouldn't miss.

They toured the tiny houses, some of them with only one room, of the first families to make their homes in Peach Leaf. And finally, they visited the antique schoolhouse, a beautiful white-and-red building with a classic bell on top. Paige knew an incredible amount of detail about the historical building's construction, its materials and the settlers who had brought it into being, and her interest in the town's past made Liam want to learn even more about the place he'd chosen to make his home. Every minute with her was a treasure, and he wanted it to last.

"You know, back then, you wouldn't have had to hide me from everyone. I would have just taken you for my bride and tossed you over my shoulder."

"Only if I didn't protest," Paige said, pointing a finger at him accusingly and trying not to laugh.

"All the same," he said, and she went silent. Her smile faded and she seemed to be far away in her own thoughts.

"Let's go to the gift shop," he said, taking her hand and changing the subject. He didn't like seeing her sad, but part of him knew he would have to keep digging until she shared more of herself with him. He wanted to know all of her—not just the person he passed in the halls at work and not just Owen's mom. He wanted everything.

After they'd purchased a few coloring books for Paige's office, Liam took her to a tiny German restaurant that was rumored to have the best Reuben sandwiches around. Upon arrival, Liam knew he'd chosen well when Paige clasped her hands and smiled.

"They have amazing food," she said. "I never get

to come here because Owen doesn't like sauerkraut or sausage, which eliminates most of the menu."

He smiled, glad to please her, and led them inside, where a hostess showed them to a table for two on the patio. The place was casually elegant and lively but not too loud. By then, the heat had calmed down, and a warm breeze blew through Paige's hair from time to time. She was beautiful and serene in the candlelight emanating from the center of the table, and her eyes shone navy blue in the twilight. Paige had worn a turquoise sundress on their date, and Liam admired the way the sun had kissed her shoulders with a shade of soft pink.

"I love this place," she said, smiling at him across the table.

"So do I," he said.

"How can you love it? Your food hasn't even come yet." They had both ordered sodas and the same sandwich, Paige's favorite.

"I don't need the food to tell me how I feel. I already know." Paige nibbled her lower lip and he could tell she was pretending to concentrate on a groove in the wood of the table.

"I love a lot of things about Peach Leaf, Paige." She looked up at him then and met his eyes over the small flame burning between them. He'd never seen anything as lovely as she was at that very moment. Everything he'd built up over the past few weeks threatened to burst inside him.

"Paige, can I ask you something?"

"Yeah, sure," she said.

"Why don't you ever talk about Mark? It sounds like he was a great guy, and it would be okay with me if you wanted to talk about him. I'm here for you for that, you know?"

She looked down at her menu and her mouth became a thin line; her brows knit together. "I guess it's probably for the same reason that you don't talk much about Callie."

"It's different, though. My wife walked out on me because I wanted kids, and she didn't, and she chose to leave rather than find a way to make things work, but your husband died. It's not the same, Paige."

She blinked at him, confused, and he realized he hadn't mentioned it before.

"You're right. It isn't the same, I guess, not really, but loss is loss. I gave Mark everything I had, and when I lost him, I lost everything. I didn't even have enough left to be a decent parent to Owen, at first." She seemed to hesitate, and Liam saw her collarbone rise and fall softly with her breathing. He hated seeing her upset, but it was important that she be able to talk to him about her past if they were ever to have a future.

He wanted one with her—he was certain of that now—but not one built on sheltered history and pain. He wanted a solid foundation for the two—*three* of them—to stand on.

"It's okay, Paige. You can talk to me. I'm here and I'm listening, and I'm not going anywhere unless you want me to."

"Probably not even then," she said and winked at him. Moisture shimmered in her eyes.

"Why don't you talk about Callie?" she asked.

He breathed in slowly and let it out.

"I guess I just want to forget about her, you know? Talking about her just brings back painful memories."

Paige grimaced. "I can definitely understand that."

"I always believed strongly that marriage is about more than just two people in love," he said, rubbing a hand over his forehead. "To me, it's also about working through things even when they're hard, even when it seems like there's no way to find common ground. Compromise, faithfulness, support, partnership...those are the things I promised to Callie when we said our vows. And even though having children was something I really, really wanted, I was willing to find a way to come to an agreement, even if that meant giving up the idea of kids."

Paige nodded, her eyes filled with what looked like a mix of seriousness and sadness. She didn't seem to be judging him; he could tell she was simply curious.

"To me, divorce was never really an option, even when we came to a crossroads," he said.

Paige furrowed her eyebrows. "But didn't Callie tell you before you got married that she didn't want kids?"

Liam closed his eyes and shook his head before looking back at Paige. "We talked about kids a few times. And maybe I wasn't listening, or maybe it was wishful thinking, or maybe I was just young and stupid, but from what I can recall of that early time together, she always seemed on board with the possibility of having children someday, in the vague way that newlyweds sometimes are. To answer your question, though—no, she never said outright that she didn't want children. And I never asked her directly, which was my mistake. Then again, I'm not sure it would have changed anything. I still loved her, and I would have done what I could to keep the marriage together."

Paige nodded, giving him the courage to continue. He hadn't talked about this to anyone, but despite his initial reluctance, sharing his pain with Paige felt...right.

"But Callie wouldn't budge on the subject, and it didn't take long before that was all we talked—*fought*—about, and it ended up wrecking both of us. Finally, she said she wanted out, and it became clear fairly quickly that there wasn't anything I could do to change her mind." Liam pulled in air and let it out slowly, trying to find the right words. "Even though she always said it was about children, I can't help believing that it was really about me. That she decided I wasn't what she wanted anymore, and the kid thing was just easier for her to say."

Unmistakable pain flashed across Paige's eyes, and it was a moment before she spoke. "Well, Liam. It was her loss to give up on someone like you."

Her words sent a flood of gratitude and affection

coursing through his veins, and before he said too much, he changed the subject back to Paige.

"I'm sure it's hard for you, too. You must miss Mark all the time."

She nodded, and he saw sincerity in her eyes, alongside a steady calm. "At first, I had the worst time with it. It was like I stopped breathing when he did." She folded and unfolded her napkin in her lap for a moment and then looked up at him. "But it's better. It's been seven months—that's a while I've had to recover. Things have gradually gotten easier for me, and I have work to keep me busy—and Owen, of course. But it's been harder on him than it has been for me."

"He's doing great, though, Paige—speaking in full sentences to me and to other kids at school— and it's because of you."

"Nonsense. You're the one I can thank for giving him his voice back." She shook her head. "I still cannot believe how far he's come in the past few weeks. I think he's really ready for Parents' Night, and I can't wait to see him up there with the other kids—having a great time, I hope," she said, offering a sad smile.

"Although you'll still be a nervous wreck."

"You've got me on that one." Paige laughed as the waitress brought their sodas. As she took a long sip of her drink, he noticed the slight unsteadiness in her hand.

"He's your child. You'll always worry about him. I know you don't want to hear it, but, even after all of this, life will still throw him blows now and then, and he'll have to have ways to cope and get through them." He had a feeling they both knew he wasn't just talking about Owen, but her, too. "The more tools he has to do that, the better off he'll be." He knew he should tell her about his weekend art-therapy group, but he wanted to make sure she would be in the right mind-set to hear him out.

"I can't thank you enough, Liam. For helping to give him those tools."

"It's not just that, though."

"Of course it is. He's clearly improved in your art classes, and he's talking to you and Jeremy and Kaylie pretty frequently now. Sure, he's not giving monologues or anything just yet, but he's getting there."

"Those are just part of it," Liam said. "The drawing and painting and sculpting are just media. He's the one who has to provide the idea, and you're the one who's given him the strength to do that."

She looked away and took another sip of her soda, hiding her emotions behind the glass.

"It's true, Paige. He's seen you open up in the past few weeks. Seeing you do what he's been afraid of has given him the confidence he needed to do the same for himself. I may have provided the tools he needed, but you provided the strength."

She stared into the bottom of her glass and stirred the ice around. Liam hoped she wouldn't hide her tears from him, should they come.

"I never told you why I was late on the first day of school, did I?" he asked. She wiped her eyes with one hand and turned away from him to dab at them with her napkin. The waitress came then and set down their food. They both thanked her, but neither moved to eat.

"I was late because I have an engagement at the hospital back in Abilene first thing on school mornings and some weekend mornings. It takes me about an hour, on good days, to get there and back. At some point, I'd really like to have a program like it at Peach Leaf Memorial, but for now, this is something I'm committed to and passionate about."

Paige looked back at him and then spread a napkin in her lap before pulling her sandwich closer.

"A program like what?" she asked, before taking a bite of her food.

"I work with an art-therapy group as part of my doctoral studies...to kids struggling with all sorts of things."

She finished chewing and her hand flew to her mouth. "Oh, my gosh," she said.

"I got that job a long time ago—well, I guess it's not really a job since I don't get paid—but the hospital's about an hour outside town. So that first day when I was late, well... You can put it together. I adore teaching, but it's the therapy part of art that's my true love and why I'm continuing to study it further. I'm in the process of trying to convince the local hospital board to consider an art-therapy program for kids like the one I run for my dissertation research. They're a little funny about the idea right now, but the director is warming up to me." He winked at Paige and then tucked into his own meal.

They ate quietly for a few moments before Paige spoke again, her voice tender.

"I'm so sorry, Liam. Truly." He held up a hand to stop her apology, but she continued. "If you'd have just told me why you were late, I would never have given you so much grief about it. I feel terrible now. How rude you must have thought I was, or maybe you still think so."

"No, Paige. I don't think you were rude at all. You had a job to do that day and you were doing it like you should. Despite my morning group, I should never have been late to work that day. The only rude one was me. And I'm sorry."

"It's okay," she said. "Truce?"

"Absolutely." He reached out and grabbed her offered hand, and instead of shaking it, he held it there, warm and soft, and caressed her fingers with his own. The gesture sent shivers through his entire body. Touching her skin felt so right to him. He wanted to hold her close for as long as he could.

"I think, once you're ready, you should maybe let Owen give the group a try. I have a hunch he'd enjoy it."

"Even though he's doing so well on his own?"

"Yes, even still. He's talking a little bit now, but he still probably has a lot to process. He lost his father. The selective mutism was just a symptom of the real problem. He's so young that he doesn't know how to manage it. For some reason, his brain has become comfortable enough lately to let up a little on the coping mechanism it gave him when his dad died. But now is when he'll be open enough to work through his emotions, and his sadness and anger at the loss might scare or overwhelm him, Paige."

Liam's words settled like lead in the bottom of Paige's chest, making it hard to take her next breath. Her first impulse was to be angry with him—but for what? For telling the truth?

She'd gone over the same information hundreds of times in her own heart, but now, hearing the same words from Liam took away some of their bite. A few weeks before, when they'd just met, she would have thought him callous and critical for implying she wasn't doing enough for her son; knowing him now, she understood that he had Owen's well-being in mind—and her own. But none of that changed the fact that she had a job to do, and there was never enough time in a day to give to Owen, much less enough for herself.

Owen. Even his name made her feel a pang of guilt that she'd left him home. Every time she thought of picking up the phone to ask a friend to take Owen for a couple of hours, she felt guilty knowing that he had only one parent left. It was the same emotion she felt now, being with Liam while Owen stayed at home with his sitter.

"Listen, Liam, I've had a great time, but I really should be getting home."

"All right, then," Liam said, and she was surprised that he didn't protest. Until she noticed the mischievous glint in his eyes. "But we're not going to your house. We're going to mine."

She opened her mouth to speak, but he interrupted before she could get any words to come out.

"Before you argue with me—and I know you will—let me just say this. You're a great mom, and Owen loves you, but he will be okay with the sitter this evening."

She started to speak, but something in his eyes pleaded with her to let him have this one, and she found herself giving up the resistance that had kept her company for the past six months. Maybe it would be okay—just this once—to let someone else take the reins for a bit.

"You're doing everything you can for him, Paige, and guess what? It's working. So take a break with me. It'll be good for both of you. Let me take you to my house for a bit, and you can sit with me and a glass of wine and just relax. For one evening, Paige. Tomorrow, if you want, you can have back all of the control, but today, let me."

His words stung a little, but he was right.

He searched her eyes across the table, and she gave him a small smile. Recalling her choice to take him to a spot designed to mask their relationship made her sandwich turn over in her stomach. She'd been dishonest with him, the person she'd become so close to, and one of the only people in whose hands she trusted her son's welfare. How dare she?

"We'll finish our sandwiches and then I'll show

you my humble abode. You can prop your feet up for a bit, Ms. Graham."

She nodded, avoiding his eyes, and they finished their dinner in near silence. It was one thing for Liam to spend time at her home. It allowed her to be there for Owen and, if anyone were to question it, she could explain Liam's time there as therapy for her son. But going to Liam's was a different step. It would be the first time she'd been away from, or not in the same building as, Owen for more than an hour or two in a long time. Before Mark's death, she'd gone on trips with girlfriends or to spend time with her sister, but she hadn't left Owen overnight since. Doing so felt like a big deal.

"Okay," she said, giving him the most genuine smile in her power. She would just have to make sure no one found out that the soon-to-be principal of Peach Leaf Elementary was going home with a member of her staff.

It was dark when Liam pulled up to Rachel's guesthouse, and Paige was secretly thankful. She had let him drive, mostly to prove that she was capable of letting go of her need to be in charge, but she wasn't sure she was ready to run into Rachel while sneaking into Liam's house.

He, however, was every bit the calm, cool man she'd come to admire, and as he opened his front door for her, she wondered why it seemed so easy for him. She could tell when he talked about his ex that he'd been brokenhearted at her leaving, yet he'd seemed fully invested in Paige, almost since the first moment she'd met him. It occurred to her that maybe it wasn't that it was easy for him; maybe, instead, he was just more willing than her to work at moving on. Maybe she could learn something from him, aside from all he had already taught her.

She walked into the living room, which was bathed in soft gold light from a table lamp beside Liam's mahogany leather sofa. The room had only a few pieces of masculine furniture, but it had an inviting, warm feeling, just like its owner. On the wall hung a few large, framed paintings. As Liam excused himself to the kitchen to get her a glass of wine, she stepped closer to study them.

The first was black and white in a simple pewter frame. Paige appreciated artwork and home decor, but the condo she shared with Owen was best described as "minimalist." She had no artistic talent to speak of and had never been very interested in making her home beautiful. She supposed it was because she'd always been happy in it, with her small family, with only simple decorations and family photographs covering the walls. But as she studied the painting on Liam's wall, she was reminded of how a piece of art could move a person deeply. This one brought to surface a sadness she didn't want to feel, made worse by the fact that it had clearly been created by a child.

"It's a little dark, I know," Liam said, coming to stand close behind her.

She wondered how long he'd been there, watching her, and she hoped he hadn't seen the way her face must mirror the painting's tone. "Yes, very," she said. "Who painted this?"

"One of the kids from my therapy group in Abilene," he answered. "It was given to me at the end of our sessions."

He didn't offer more, and Paige hesitated to ask, but she had to know what would cause such pain in a young person.

"What happened to him?" Liam seemed to consider briefly whether or not he should tell her, but then he looked at her, his eyes intense.

"Her mom was a police officer, and sadly, she was killed in the line of duty. Angela painted this in a class when I was a student teacher, very early in the year."

"I see." Paige understood now that he'd been reluctant to dredge up her own emotions. She was touched by the kind tenderness of his discretion.

"She had a happy ending, though. I watched her work through her pain every week in class, and as she put her hurt onto paper and into clay, it seeped out of her. And by the end of the semester, her work became brighter, as did Angela."

Liam studied her face as he handed Paige her wine. She wondered if he could see the questions there.

"It's not that easy for everyone. Each person I work with, and each person in the world, has his or her own way of dealing with grief. But losing someone never means that the world has ended, even though it may feel like that at times. There is always a way to work through it, and there is always something worth the effort on the other side."

Paige took a sip of her chilled wine so that he couldn't see the tears forming behind her eyes. It was white, sweet and cheap—her favorite. He must have remembered from their brief time in the wine aisle of Peach Leaf Produce. It tasted even better for the coffee mug he'd served it in. That made her smile, and her tears receded.

"Sorry about the cup," he said. "My real dining ware is still in storage. I figured there wasn't much need to unpack until I found a place of my own, until I decided whether or not I planned to stay."

A lump formed in her throat and she struggled to form words around it. "Do you? Plan to stay?"

"Well, that depends…"

"On what?"

"On whether or not I'm wanted here and not just needed," he answered. Paige didn't miss the solemnity in his voice.

"It's a beautiful piece," she said, changing the subject. She buried her face in the mug and took another sip. She hoped it would calm her nerves and cool the scalding blood pulsing through her. "Do you do any painting yourself?"

She could see the disappointment in his expression, and it shot straight through her chest. She had refused to answer the question he'd all but asked. They were both dancing around their true feelings, and Paige was starting to wonder if she might explode at the palpable heat between them.

If he made one move to touch her, she would come undone all over again. Oddly, for a person who always wanted to have the upper hand, she found herself desperate for him to take control, like he had that first time. She wanted him to lead her to his bedroom, and she knew, with everything inside her, that if he did, he would take care of her like he had before—and she would be okay.

But was she ready to be taken care of in the long run? For the rest of her life, even? She could taste freedom that wasn't yet hers, and part of her wanted to dive into it and let go completely.

"I draw some," he said, and motioned for her to follow him. He led her down a small hallway and stopped at a door, turning to face her. "If I let you in there, you have to promise to be gentle, okay?"

"What do you mean?"

"Just promise."

"Okay, fine," she said, rolling her eyes. "I promise."

He paused briefly, as if second-guessing his decision to let her into the room, and then he took a deep breath and opened the door. The room's walls were almost entirely glass.

"This used to be a greenhouse," he said, "before my great-aunt had the front area added on and turned it into a guesthouse."

"It's lovely," she said. She looked up and could see the night sky above her through the glass ceiling, just like at the gallery. She sucked in a delighted breath and Liam smiled, watching her.

And then, as her eyes traveled around, she noticed that instead of plants, she was surrounded by drawings. They were absolutely everywhere—on shelves, on tables and in standing-up bunches on the floor. Most of them were done in plain gray, but several were clearly drawn with colored pencils. All of them were marvelous.

Without words, she left Liam standing by the door and made her way around the room, stopping to examine each one closely before moving on to the next. Most of them were landscapes and tall buildings. She picked out the Eiffel Tower, Big Ben and the Washington Monument. The rest were fascinating images that must have come from the recesses of his mind.

"These are all yours?"

Liam nodded. His expression was a mix of shyness and poorly hidden joy.

"I've never shown this stuff to anyone...I've cared about...before," he said. "It's nice, though. Unless of course you're standing there thinking I'm the worst person in the world to have ever picked up a pencil..."

Paige laughed at Liam's easy joke about himself. She was immensely flattered.

"Why am I the first to see these pieces?" The wine must have been doing its job because the leaden fear she'd had upon entering the house was all but completely diminished and had been replaced by a rich sense of comfort. Owen was home safe with his babysitter, and here she was, with an extremely good-looking, charming man who was pure gold at his center. Maybe that's what it felt like to lose oneself in someone else. She'd forgotten, but Liam seemed set on reminding her.

"I'm not sure," he said. "I guess I just never saw my own art as all that important. I never had any interest in becoming a professional artist myself. Don't get me wrong—the money is nice when I sell a piece. I just didn't give in completely to that life. I've always been more interested in the ways art can help people, but I love to draw and paint, so I do it for myself in my spare time. And now I'm sharing it with you."

"You've been to all of these places?"

"Some of them. Others are drawn from photographs I've received from friends. It's soothing for me. Concentrating on the lines and shading gives me space to think."

"That must be your secret, then," she said, nudging him softly with her elbow.

"Secret to what?"

"Staying so calm all the time."

"Everyone needs an outlet sometimes, Paige. You can't keep all the stress and the pain locked away inside all the time. It has to come out or it eats you up eventually."

"Is that how you deal with your own demons?"

He nodded. "When I was young, my father wanted me to be just like him. He didn't want me to be an art teacher or an art therapist, or anything other than an oil tycoon like himself. And I saw what it did to our family. My dad was away all the time, and my mom missed him constantly. He was never a real part of Rachel's and my life, other than to tell us what he thought of our choices whenever he did happen to be home. He thought I was wasting my time on a career path that would never lead to much financial gain. I tried many times to tell him that it didn't matter, that art and teaching made me happy, but none of that meant anything to him. What I never understood, though, is why he cared so much about wealth when he and Mom were never happy, in spite of all that money."

Paige listened to him talk, her heart aching for Liam the same way it did for Owen. How had she not seen it earlier? Both of them had experienced great loss, and both of them hurt because of it. But somehow, Liam had still managed to find something he dearly loved and had made a life for himself where he obviously thrived. Her heart filled with hope that her son would be able to do the same.

"And did it help with what happened with Callie?"

"Yes, I think so," he said, and then sipped his own wine. "She'd made up her mind and there wasn't a damn thing I could've done about it. If she had been wrong, I would have fought for her. But she wanted something I couldn't give her, so I let her go when she wanted to go. It was best for both of us. Her leaving me was not my fault."

Paige saw a new intensity in Liam's eyes as he opened his heart to her. He was giving her the deepest parts of himself, the stuff she continually refused to give him.

"Just as Mark's death was not your fault, Paige. You need to know that, once and for all."

Hearing the truth wasn't the same as letting it seep into her veins. She wondered if she would feel that way for the rest of her life; if she had changed one thing about the last morning she saw her husband alive, would anything be different now? She knew she wasn't responsible for his death, but would she ever be able to let go of him the way Liam had Callie? Liam was right. It wasn't the same, but she knew she would have to make peace with it and move forward if she and Owen were ever to have a chance at a new life.

Paige held her breath as she watched Liam set his mug on a shelf and slowly walk toward her. She could see his heart in his eyes; they burned into hers with a force that made her hands shake until he took her drink from her hands and set it next to his.

He turned back to her and pushed the hair away from her eyes. He cupped her face in his hands, running his thumbs beneath her eyes. She knew he could feel the tears that had slipped out against her will, yet he didn't seem to mind. Pushing them aside, he pulled her lips against his.

She closed her eyes and allowed him to draw her in, her heart pounding with passion fiercer than any she'd ever known, and as he ran his tongue softly along her lips, she willed herself not to simply dissolve in his embrace. She let him push past her lips, and as he deepened the kiss, she knew she'd fallen hard for him.

She'd finally let herself go, and the feeling was beyond any perfection she could have imagined.

Chapter Nine

"Ready to head back home to meet up with your mom, buddy?"

Liam turned to Owen. The two stood side by side in Liam's room at the hospital, washing paintbrushes together.

"Yep, and we're going for ice cream, right? Like you said?"

"Of course we're going for ice cream. But first I have to find a place to live," Liam answered, laughing softly at the kid's eagerness.

"But you already have a place to live at Ms. Rachel's."

Liam grinned at his little shadow and resisted the impulse to reach down and hug Owen with his sudsy wet hands. It was his first day in Liam's therapy class, and Owen had fit right in with the other kids. Liam breathed a sigh of relief, knowing that he would have good news to report back to Paige.

He thought of her as he dried their hands and thought back to that night two weeks ago. If he lingered too long on that memory, as he had too many times throughout the day, he could recall the way her mouth had tasted as she'd kissed him back and the hungry way she'd opened up to him, finally, and seemed to have given him her whole heart. She had refused to stay the night and he'd driven her home rather late, but Owen had not woken up.

He knew Paige was still funny about being seen out with him, and she'd made sure that every date was planned with as little likelihood of running into people she knew as possible. She'd done everything but suggest they only date in the next town over, and he knew she would have if it hadn't been more than thirty miles away. He understood and was trying to be patient with her, but soon enough she'd have to decide what was most important to her— her image as the new potential principal, or Liam's place in her life.

He thought back to the call from the Peach Leaf Memorial Hospital director earlier that day. Liam's professor and boss at the hospital in Abilene had spoken with the director at Peach Leaf's hospital and vouched for Liam's successful program. Apparently, the Peach Leaf Memorial director wanted to start a similar initiative at his institution. He couldn't wait to tell Paige about the offer to start an art-therapy program there for patients. Though Liam hadn't gone so far as to say as much, he would gladly give up the art teacher job, both for this new opportunity and for Paige—that is, if she wanted him to. And the proximity meant he wouldn't have to drive to Abilene anymore, and Owen could get the same continued therapy at a much closer location. He just had to make sure Paige was on board.

He still couldn't really see why anyone finding out about their romance continued to bother her so much. Life was too short to worry so much about appearances.

Liam held up Owen's backpack so the boy could put his arms through the straps, and then he locked the classroom door and they headed out to his truck. With Paige, Owen and the hospital offer, it seemed like the stars had finally aligned for him. He had almost everything he'd ever wanted.

He struggled to trust it, from time to time, but he wouldn't allow himself to go down a negative path. He was ready for good things in his life, and he wasn't about to stop his lucky stars from doing their best.

If he held on, Paige would trust it too, soon enough. She had to—he couldn't give her up. The two of them had faced too much loss, and in his mind, they deserved a heavy dose of happiness.

"Mom!" Owen called out, waving at Paige as they stepped out onto the sidewalk in downtown Peach Leaf some time later. The afternoon sunshine melted the air-conditioned chill from their skin as Liam lifted his chin to let warmth hit his face.

"I think you may be the only person I know who wants to bask in this heat," Paige said to Liam.

He leaned down to kiss her cheek. She was adorable in a white linen top and slim yellow jeans. It was turning into a perfect day.

Liam had kept quiet about his surprise at Paige's willingness to let Owen ride with him all the way to Abilene, but he couldn't deny how great it felt to know she trusted him with the most important person in her life.

"Shall we, then?" he asked, ignoring the way her eyes darted about after he'd kissed her and the way his bright mood darkened slightly because of it. Paige pushed a button and her vehicle's lock sounded. Liam got Owen settled in the backseat of his truck and Paige in front.

Give it time, he thought. *Just give it time.*

He just hoped it wouldn't be too long. He'd found the family he wanted, and he saw no reason to wait for life with them to begin.

He had a list of three houses he wanted to see, but Liam was pretty sure which one he was going to pick before he even laid eyes on any of them. The first one they pulled up to was a town house near downtown Peach Leaf, across the street from the old library. He liked the idea of being able to walk over and grab a book when the mood hit, and there was a perfect park nearby, with a walking trail surrounding a duck pond.

He loved traveling to see the world's great cities, but there was a charm to places like Peach Leaf.

Once he'd gotten past the idea that just about everybody could get into his business in this small town if they were so inclined, he'd been surprised how easy he warmed to its cozy, comforting feel. He liked the way Ms. Hays at the grocery store had ordered his favorite coffee when she'd discovered him searching the shelves for it in vain, and he looked forward to the farmer's market downtown every weekend, where he could buy fresh food that tasted like it had been grown with care. People were friendly and genuinely hospitable in a way that he hadn't experienced in other places he'd lived, and he was getting used to the idea of making his home there.

"Wow." Paige sucked in a breath beside him and he studied her face as she saw the town house for the first time. It was his second choice of the three he'd narrowed the Realtor's list down to.

"You like this one, huh?" he asked.

"It's adorable," she said.

"Don't say that for everyone to hear. It's going to be a bachelor pad for a while. Though not for too long, I hope."

She tried not to, but Liam saw the shy smile playing at the corners of her mouth. *Good.* Maybe they were getting closer to being on the same page.

"Where's the Realtor?" she asked, glancing around the street at the nearby cars.

"He'll be here soon. We're a little bit early. I figured we could walk around a bit, check out what's nearby."

"I've been past this place a thousand times, but

I've never really noticed it before as a house, you know. I always thought it was another historical building or something."

Liam grinned, pleased to see Paige noticing her town in a new way. He knew sometimes the best way to see your own city was through someone else's eyes; because she'd grown up there, Paige probably never thought much about the old buildings she'd seen regularly since she was a child.

"You'd be right," he said. "It is a historical building. The foundation was poured in the 1800s and it began as a small general store. The owner lived upstairs in an apartment and ran the shop from the ground floor. Then, when the town started to grow and the owner aged, he sold it as two separate apartments. Now, it's a regular house, but there's still a stairwell on the outside. The Realtor informed me that I shouldn't worry—there aren't two kitchens or anything like that. It's been remodeled and updated so now it's a normal house, with two bedrooms upstairs and two down."

"I'm impressed," Paige said, smiling up at him, her eyebrows raised teasingly. "Someone did his research. If you ever have a downslide in your art skills, I'll be sure to let the history department know you're quite the know-it-all."

He laughed, happy to see her in such a playful mood. Liam had fallen in love with every aspect of Paige's character, but nothing compared to seeing a smile spread across her face.

"Are there any secret passageways?" Owen asked.

"I don't think so, buddy, but who knows? There may be one that no one's found yet. You'll have to check it out when we go inside.

The three of them bought bread at a small drugstore and walked across to the park, where Owen fed the ducks until it was time to meet the Realtor. Liam went to greet him as Paige and Owen went back to his car to put the rest of the bread away.

"Mr. Campbell," the Realtor said, shaking Liam's hand. "Good afternoon to you. I know this isn't your first choice, but wait until you see the inside."

"Give me just a moment, Mr. Samuels," Liam said. "I've brought some company with me." Liam heard Owen and Paige coming up the steps to join them, but when he turned to introduce them, he saw the color drain rapidly from Paige's face.

"Is something wrong?" he asked, reaching out for her hand.

She stared past him at the Realtor, her face the color of paper.

"Well, Ms. Graham!" Tom Samuels said cheerfully. "I didn't know I'd be running into you."

Paige wiped her hands on her jeans as she found her voice. "Hello, Tom. How are you?"

Liam's eyes darted from Paige to his Realtor. "Did I miss something? How do you two know each other? Paige, did Tom help you find your condo?"

"Well, yes, actually, that's part of it, but..." she said slowly. Liam was at a complete loss for why she looked so nervous she might jump out of her skin.

"Paige and my wife go way back," the Realtor

said. "They've worked together for years. How many has it been now, honey? Must be going on eight at least?"

Liam was still confused as he met Paige's eyes, searching them for clues.

She swallowed and he saw Owen look up at Paige with nervous eyes as she squeezed her son's hand. "Liam, Tom is Principal Matthews's husband."

"Oh, I see. Well, that makes perfect sense," he said, hoping that neither of them would hear the slight jolt in his voice as he struggled over the words. He needed to keep calm about this new development, to keep his confidence for both him and Paige and to show her she had no need to worry. But he couldn't even convince himself of that, as he stood silent, trying to come up with a reason why she would be house hunting with him.

"And how do you two know each other?" Mr. Samuels asked.

Right. The man had no idea. Liam had only spoken to the Realtor briefly about what might interest him. They hadn't yet sat down and talked finances or any details, so Mr. Samuels didn't know that Liam was a teacher at Peach Leaf. Paige's eyes seemed to beg him not to say anything, and a knot formed in his stomach as he searched for how to answer.

He didn't agree with her that they had anything to hide, so why did he suddenly sympathize with Paige and have the urge to lie? It would be easy to make up something—*anything*—but the truth would come out in less than a week, when the entire faculty and staff of Peach Leaf Elementary got together for the principal's going-away dinner at the school's auditorium and everyone saw them together. In a small town like this, even if he didn't touch her all night, people would just know. If he remained silent about their relationship now, he would only delay the inevitable. Liam just hoped Paige was working through the same thought process as they stood there, saying nothing. Their speechlessness itself was a red flag that something was wrong, and Mr. Samuels did not seem to overlook the tension.

Liam cleared his throat. "We know each other from work. I'm the new art teacher at the elementary school." Paige sent a grateful look his way. Owen stared up at her and then looked at Liam, as if trying to decipher the strange behavior going on among the adults.

Mr. Samuels nodded, and Liam saw the exact moment when the realization hit him. He was surprised to see that the Realtor only gave it a second's thought. When he spoke again, nothing in his tone indicated any concern. "Well, I didn't realize. My wife speaks very highly of all of her teachers, and that includes both of you."

Paige looked up at Liam then with a frigid expression.

"Shall we get on inside?" Mr. Samuels said, glancing back and forth between them. "I think you'll just love it."

After the awkward situation with Principal Matthews's husband, they had somehow managed to get through the rest of the day without incident. Paige longed to head home, to soak in a hot bath and just forget about the embarrassment of running into Mr. Samuels. She should have put two and two together when Liam had told her the Realtor's name the day before, but she had always known him by his first name, Tom, which was how he wanted to be addressed any time she had seen him. She supposed she'd known at some point that Ms. Matthews had kept her maiden name, but she'd been having such a good time with Liam that it hadn't occurred to her that day.

That's what can happen when you're not careful, she chided herself. She was upset with Liam for not keeping quiet about his job when he'd had the chance, but the anger welling up inside her seemed way too strong for the circumstances. Her body tingled with the pent-up stress of the past few weeks. Principal Matthews's dinner was coming up, and Paige had a strong feeling that her boss would use the opportunity to announce Paige as her successor, with every teacher in the school there to hear. Paige should have had her head on straight; she should have been ever more careful in the weeks leading up to the event. Instead, she'd allowed Liam to convince her that she didn't have anything to worry about, and she'd gotten careless in the process.

"Paige, talk to me," Liam said next to her. They were seated in a booth at the old-fashioned general store. Owen happily dug into his ice cream sundae, but Paige hadn't touched the one Liam had ordered for the two of them to share. She stared into it, not answering him, as if the solution to all of her problems might be found in the creamy dessert. If only.

He sighed heavily and picked up his spoon to take another bite. He smiled at Owen's chocolate-covered chin. "You've got a little something here," he said, pointing to his own face. Owen giggled and picked up his napkin to wipe away the mess.

The scene would have normally made her smile, too. Until an hour earlier, it had almost felt like the three of them were a family.

"Paige, I'll be outside," he said, whispering close to her ear so Owen wouldn't worry. "I don't think you should let this bother you so much. You're all worked up about something that isn't a big deal."

She clenched her teeth and forced herself to smile across the table, avoiding Liam's face as he turned from her and walked out to the patio area of the store.

"Owen, honey? See that window there?"

"Yeah, Mom," her son said, glancing away from his treat just long enough to see where she pointed.

"Mr. Campbell and I will be just out there, okay? I'll be able to see you, and you can come out if anything happens, all right?"

"Sure, Mom," he said, tucking back into his ice cream.

She rose from the booth and bent down to kiss his soft hair before she joined Liam outside. Taking a deep breath, she sat across from him at the picnic table he'd chosen.

"Paige…"

"You had no right to tell Tom Samuels that we work together. What if he goes straight home and tells her?"

"It's okay, Paige. He didn't even seem to care about it. You're the only person who was upset about us being together."

She shook her head. "Why can't you get it? Don't you know the risk you're taking every time we step out a door together? Why doesn't all of this bother you?

"Because it doesn't matter, Paige. It's not that important."

"How can you say that? You could lose your job if the right people find out that we're...whatever it is we're doing. I could lose my job. And if I lose that, I lose everything I've worked for...for Owen. I've let things go too far, and now I don't know what to do."

"How often do you think this sort of thing happens?" Liam gripped the table and leaned toward her.

She blinked at him, trying hard not to focus on the pain she found in his eyes. Her chest tightened and she pulled in air to quell the feeling. She knew exactly how many times this sort of thing happened—for her, at least. Twice. Once with Mark, and again, miraculously, with Liam. What an injustice it was that the one person she wanted to be with was off-limits. She'd ignored that very fact in spite of her full comprehension of the repercussions, and now she would have to pay for it. She couldn't have everything she wanted, after all. How silly of her to think she ever would be able to handle single motherhood, her job and a relationship. How silly to think she could fall in love again and not face the consequences.

"I don't want to talk about this," she said. "Especially not with Owen here."

Something that looked markedly like disappointment flooded Liam's face. She knew he was getting tired of hearing her say the same thing. It had been selfish of her to string him along all this time, playing into their shared fantasy of a life together. "Can you just take Owen and me back? We have the dinner this weekend and I want to get some rest."

Liam nodded, and she knew that it was because of Owen that he didn't push her further. It was because of Owen that they'd met and because of Owen that they had been able to spend so much time together, under the guise of helping her son get better.

But it wasn't because of Owen that she'd allowed herself to do the one thing she was so afraid of.

She was in love with Liam Campbell. No amount of her usual resistance was going to get her out of it.

Paige just wondered how many more times she would use her son as an excuse not to let Liam get any closer than he already had.

Liam, to whom she would have to lie by saying she simply wasn't interested in getting to know him any further.

Hopefully, for both their sakes, he would believe her.

Chapter Ten

"Okay, honey. Make sure you do your homework before you play with Kaylie and Jeremy," Paige said. "And make sure you do what Ms. Rachel says. I want a good report when I get back."

Rachel laughed as Owen tucked himself under her arm. "I'm sure we'll be just fine," she said. "You two have a great time."

"We will," Paige said. She hurried to her car in front of Rachel's house. She wanted to get out of there before Liam saw her from the guesthouse. It had been hard enough trying to explain to Rachel why the two of them had chosen not to ride together—or rather, she had chosen not to.

Liam had wanted to drive her, but Paige had re-fused. The faculty had all been invited to the school for dinner that night, and Paige didn't want to risk being seen driving there with him. Before that day at the ice cream shop, the past few weeks with Liam had been equal parts amazing and hard on her. They had spent so much time together. Liam often brought pizza to her home and helped Owen with homework, not to mention their precious, stolen moments alone, and she had finally agreed to bring Owen to one of Liam's Saturday morning art-therapy groups.

She couldn't have been more thankful. The group was small and intimate. The kids had seemed to accept Owen; he was doing beautifully, talking more easily and making friends. Liam had described some of the art projects to Paige. She had been to his classroom at the hospital to see some of Owen's work herself and had been amazed at the pieces the kids had created.

Aside from Owen's paintings and sculptures, she'd seen pieces that made her heart ache with their intensity and maturity. And though she'd asked, Liam had been clear that he couldn't give her any information into the current patients themselves, other than showing her their work. He kept everything confidential except when it was related to Owen. She was proud to know that he was doing so much better, but she knew she had Liam to thank.

Liam had explained that the art projects helped Owen to express things that he had trouble finding words for, deep-set emotions that he might not know how to articulate otherwise. Paige accepted it, but she still wished that Owen would open up to her about how he'd felt when he lost his dad. Partly it was because she wanted to talk about Mark herself and still seemed unable to. She'd had some of her own therapy alongside Owen, but she'd never been able to connect with any of the doctors enough to do any good. After a few quiet sessions, she'd stopped trying and had resigned herself to the fact that she just couldn't do it. It hurt too much to talk about her husband and the life they'd shared.

Strangely, though, she sometimes had the feeling that she might want to talk to Liam about it even more than she already had, but they hadn't exactly had much time to themselves. He had talked to her in passing at school over the past few days and had called several times—all of which she'd ignored, too afraid to face her fear. Paige knew he could see right through her thin excuses when she said she was too busy. She knew that he was aware she didn't want to be seen with him in public. In Peach Leaf, each time they went out meant possibly running into someone from school. That someone could inform Principal Matthews that her top choice for the job was dating a faculty member, and her chance would be gone in an instant. She couldn't afford the risk. But she knew Liam was becoming impatient, and she didn't know how much longer she could keep it up. She still couldn't figure out why it didn't seem to matter as much to him. He knew the outcome as well as she did, yet he didn't seem as concerned.

She pulled into the school parking lot behind several other cars and checked her mirror to check that

Liam wasn't behind her. She hadn't discussed this evening with him, other than to decline his offer to drive her. He'd been unhappy enough about that, and she didn't want to push him any further for fear she might succeed in turning him away entirely. She was exasperated at her inner conflict. Her heart was tired of hiding her feelings for him from the world.

She parked her car and headed inside, feeling silly in her dress. It was deep blue and one-shouldered. She'd bought it last weekend when she hadn't been able to find anything more sensible, though she knew she hadn't overdressed because the evening included a four-course meal and, knowing Principal Matthews, would include fine wine and dessert. She still felt out of her element. She was used to being simple and professional. It had been years since she'd dressed up for anything. The last time had been a formal function for Mark's firehouse.

She recalled the sparkly black dress and elegant heels she'd worn. Paige was surprised to find that the memory brought only a smile and none of the sadness she usually felt when she thought about Mark. She knew she could attribute the change to Liam's presence in her life.

She stopped and sat on a bench outside the building to collect her thoughts. It was *Liam* she'd thought of when she'd chosen the dress. Liam to whom she now ran when she had a concern about Owen. Liam with whom she wanted to spend the rest of her life and build a *family...*

"Hey, sweetheart. You look divine."

Cam's loud cheery voice clamored into Paige's thoughts. She looked down at her body and had to agree with her best friend. The navy dress she'd picked out was a little more daring than what she would usually wear, with its deep V-neck, sexy but still appropriate, and the sparkly heels that made her feel tall and confident. She'd swiped on a little mascara, a little blush and a sheer, red-tinted lip gloss at the last minute, and the results were...nice.

She couldn't help thinking that, if she were with Liam, she would do this more often. He made her feel beautiful without any of the extra stuff, but dressing up like this reminded her of one of the fun things about being a woman. In the past months, she'd forgotten that, and it was nice to remember.

"You don't look too bad yourself," Paige said, winking at her best friend.

"What's up with you, honey? You look like your dog died."

Paige did her best to smile convincingly, but she wasn't feeling up to hiding. She wanted Cam to reach out and wrap her in a big hug. She wanted to cry into her shoulder and tell her everything that had been going on the past few weeks with Liam. Instead, she forced her features into an arrangement that she hoped made it look like she was happy to be at the dinner. "It's nothing really."

Cam wasn't buying it. "Is it nerves about tonight? Because you have nothing to worry about. Everybody's super excited about you being the new principal."

Even though it had been her goal, Paige felt sick that she'd fooled Cam.

"How did you know?"

"In this town?" Cam tilted her head to the side and looked quizzically at Paige. "We all love Principal Matthews, but everyone thinks it will be good to have someone, well, younger in charge, you know, to shake things up a bit."

"Ha! You're looking at the wrong person then."

Cam grabbed Paige by the shoulders and stared straight into her face. She'd never seen her friend with anything close to the seriousness that covered her features now.

"No way. In all seriousness, Paige, we all truly respect the work you've done to get this far. None of us is a better teacher, and that will be what makes you a great principal. You know all of this, though, deep down in there." Cam poked a finger into Paige's breast and they both laughed. "I mean in your heart," she said. "Now get your butt in there."

"Cam," she said, working to gather the right words for what she was about to say.

She'd realized it a long time ago, but she'd never dared to tell anyone, including herself. "I don't want to be principal. I don't want to be in charge."

Her best friend sat beside her on the bench and was uncharacteristically quiet for a long moment before she spoke. "Why, honey? You'd be so great at it."

"I miss teaching, but more than that, I've come to realize that I miss having more time to be there for Owen," Paige answered. She felt the floodgates open

and everything she'd been holding on to poured out
in a rush of tears. Cam moved fast to pull a tissue
out of her tiny purse. Paige accepted it and wiped
her eyes, careful to avoid smudging the mascara she
rarely wore and regretted now. She saw the black liquid in the tissue and knew she would look terrible
when she was called up to make a speech. Everyone
would expect her to look happy and gracious at the
job offer. She prayed she would be able to fake what
they all wanted to see.

"Oh, sweetheart. I had no idea. Why didn't you
tell me this a long time ago? Why didn't you tell
Principal Matthews?"

Why hadn't she told Liam?

"I have to take this job. I need this job." She closed
her eyes and nodded her head, as though the physical
movement might somehow convince her.

"No, you don't." Cam got up from her seat and
knelt in front of Paige. She took another tissue from
her purse and wiped at Paige's face. Cam placed a
finger under her chin and met her eyes. "You don't
need this job. If you don't want it, don't take it."

Paige shook her head. "It's not that simple. I have
to think about Owen."

Cam's gaze drifted downward. "Paige, Owen is
all you ever think about. Everyone can see that. He's
your world. And although I know you're a fantastic
mom to him, well, maybe you need to start thinking
about how to be a little better to yourself."

Paige looked up and saw the sincere concern in
Cam's knitted brows and firmly set mouth.

"I don't have time to be good to the both of us, Cam. I'm so scared that if I let up on Owen, something will happen, and I'm all he has left."

"That was true until…"

"Until what?" Paige sniffled. There was no hope of repairing the mess she knew she'd find her face in at the first sight of a mirror. She would have to go up in front of all those people, Liam included, looking like a terrible mess.

"You know what. Until Liam came along."

Paige's mouth went dry. "So, you knew about that?"

"Well, yeah. I had my suspicion that there was something going on between the two of you. I mean, you know…more than possibly what should be in your situation."

"Do you think anyone else knows about us? If anyone finds out, it could be really awful."

Cam bit her lip and her eyes narrowed. "That could be. There's really no way around that. To answer your question, no, I don't think anyone else knows. I know," she said, covering her heart with a hand, "but that's because I'm your best friend, and it's my job to know things like that, even if you don't tell me." Paige felt guilt knot up in her chest. She opened her mouth to apologize, but Cam continued.

"And yeah, if you don't do something about this whole thing soon, the wrong people might find out about it, and Liam might have to find another position. But think about it, Paige. How many teaching jobs are out there as opposed to how many great men are out there?"

Paige's eyebrows rose. "You have a point, but it doesn't fix anything."

"Of course it doesn't. But life is rarely that easy," Cam said and reached out to grab Paige's hand with her own. "You know that better than anyone, I think."

The tears Paige had dried threatened to return. After all this time, she still wasn't ready to talk at length about losing Mark. Yet it was different somehow, since Liam had been around. She knew in the very depths of her heart that she had grieved Mark's death, and that she was ready to move on, but for some reason, she couldn't get to the point where she was ready to talk a lot about him again, to keep his memory alive. She wanted it to be black-and-white. If he was gone, then he was gone. She wasn't yet prepared to resurrect his memory in casual conversation. She thought suddenly of Owen; the two of them hadn't talked about Mark at all. By keeping herself from talking about his father, she was keeping him from remembering the time that they had as a family. She was sacrificing all the good things to keep out the pain from the bad. And she wasn't the only one affected by her choice.

"My point is, Paige, now is the time for you to decide what it is that you want for your future. You lost your husband, yes, and no one will ever replace him, but at the same time, you're still young, and you still deserve love, and it's been long enough. You don't owe Mark any more of your sadness. You owe it to him to let yourself love again. He would have wanted you happy and you know it. And Owen could use a man in his life in the future. And I can think of a good one." Cam nudged Paige's shoulder and they both laughed.

"So you're not mad at me about keeping it a secret?"

"No, I'm not mad. Just do me a favor and keep your best friend in the loop from now on. Okay?"

"Agreed."

"We'd better get in there before Matthews thinks you bailed on her and makes the mistake of putting me in charge." Cam's eyebrows shot up and her eyes sparkled with her mischievous smile. "Yikes! What a disaster that would be."

Paige laughed and smoothed her dress, which was considerably wrinkled from the bench. She would have to do some major damage control in the bathroom to make any sort of reasonable impression up there.

They walked arm in arm into the school and were escorted to the auditorium, which had somehow transformed into a sort of ballroom. The seats had been removed and tables were set up with soft gold cloths covering them, and a stage area had been set up with a microphone that made Paige's heart race.

What was she going to say up there? What *could* she say? She owed it to Principal Matthews to take the position. She had allowed her boss to think that she was happy and honored to be considered, and she hadn't once wavered in any way. It would come as a complete shock to her now if Paige decided to back down. And there was no way she could be honest about what had changed her mind. The principal was still in charge, and if she chose, she could take Liam's job if she found out about them. The school had a strict policy about supervisors dating their staff, and Paige had her own reasons to consider on top of it.

She thought back to that night with her father all those years ago. He'd come home so late, and as far as Paige knew, her mom had never suspected anything. It must have been devastating for her mother when her father confronted her about his affair. Their family had been a rock in the town. All of Paige's life, people had commented on how happy her parents seemed, how great they were together, until her father had destroyed everything with his behavior. Shame heated her face just thinking about it. Imagine if people found out what she was hiding. It would bring up her father's scandal all over again. It didn't matter that years had passed, or that in her case the apple had not only fallen far from the tree, but it had rolled miles away. Everyone in town knew her father's story.

She couldn't bear the thought of reliving it.

She managed to tidy herself up to "presentable" status with a quick trip to the bathroom. She'd put on a fresh coat of gloss and mascara. Paige knew she looked decent enough to make an appearance, but no amount of makeup could fix the fact that she had no idea what she was going to say if she was called up to speak.

She looked around for Liam. He had said he would be there just a few minutes after her. She knew they couldn't exactly embrace in front of everyone, but she would have felt a hundred times better just knowing he was in the audience to catch her should she fall.

And falling was a very strong possibility.

She stood at the back of the room, watching her colleagues file in. She knew she should be sociable, but her usual drive eluded her that evening.

"Are you ready, my dear?" The familiar voice startled her and she jumped before she could stop herself.

"Principal Matthews! So good to see you." Her boss looked radiant and incredibly calm—the opposite of how Paige was feeling. She wore a simple, finely cut black dress and red peep-toe heels.

"You're awfully jumpy. Is anything the matter?"

"No, everything's fine. Just nervous, is all."

"You're not getting cold feet now, are you?" The older woman's tone was joking, but Paige caught the hint of warning behind it. They both had something to lose if Paige decided not to take the job. Plenty of people would be standing in line if Paige declined the position, but it would be difficult to choose another person on such short notice. The new semester was only a few months away.

Paige was grateful when she heard music start up so she didn't have to give an answer.

"Why don't you go have some fun, darling? We'll have a chance to talk later, won't we?"

Her boss gave Paige a smile and patted her shoulder before going to mingle with the other faculty and staff. Everyone from school was there. Everyone would see her falter. She had to find Liam for support. He was the only person who could make her feel better about the whole thing, and he might be able to help her decide what to do. Paige pulled out her phone and texted Rachel to see if she might know where Liam was, and she breathed a sigh of relief when she got an answer.

As Ms. Matthews walked away, Paige glanced around her to be sure no one was watching, and as soon as she could, she slipped away from the crowd.

He managed to sneak into the school without anyone noticing. He probably looked like a janitor as he parked in the back and took the side door, dressed in his favorite old jeans and a work shirt. His classroom was dark, though he could hear the music and din of laughter and talking coming from over in the auditorium. Paige would be there, he knew, and she would look amazing, her shy beauty outshining every other woman in the room. That was only one of many things he regretted about doing this. He would probably never get to see her in a gown. He would see her around town, sure, but things wouldn't be the same.

He began opening drawers and cabinets and placing his supplies into the cardboard boxes he'd brought from home. Plenty had been left over from his move to Rachel's, where it looked like he would be staying for a while. He'd gotten the call from the

Peach Leaf Memorial hospital director the day before, with news that the facility was offering him a full-time art-therapist position. He would have his own office and a studio classroom in the psychiatric wing. The director had assured him that he would be compensated well, like any other therapist, once he completed his Ph.D. He only had a few more credits to go and Peach Leaf Memorial was fully willing to cover the rest of his tuition. It was the career he'd dreamed of since he'd gotten his bachelor's degree, and he was more than ready for it to begin. He almost had everything he'd ever wanted.

Just one thing was missing...well, make that two. He had tried several times to talk to Paige since they'd fought at the ice cream shop, but she'd made it clear she didn't want anything to do with him, or at least it seemed that way. It destroyed him that he couldn't tell her about this new job. His joy was cut in half because he couldn't watch her face light up at the news. And the worst part was, it would seemingly fix everything. It would keep him out of the school so that she wouldn't have to be concerned about their relationship anymore.

Yes, it would look like everything was okay. But he had seen enough patients in his art-therapy group to know better. He needed more from her than just knowing she wouldn't pull away from him if he kissed her in public. Paige might not know it yet, but she was using that excuse to cover up deeper problems. He'd spent a lot of time thinking about it, and he knew that she had definitely made peace with her husband's death, but she wasn't comfortable enough to talk about his life, rather than his death. Liam knew he could never replace Mark, but he also refused to pretend that Owen's father hadn't existed. If he was going to be a part of Owen's and Paige's lives, he needed to know that she could talk to her son about his father. He wouldn't let the kid grow up not knowing that he had once had a dad who sounded like he'd been a great guy. It wasn't good for either of them. And he needed for Paige to sort that out on her own. He wasn't going to push her anymore.

Liam pulled the last few paintings off his walls, rolled them up and carefully wrapped rubber bands around them. He would probably have to rent a warehouse someday to hold all of his students' art, but even after he saw them get well, he could never bear to get rid of any of it. Each piece was part of a path to someone's healing, and many of them had been given to him. It was a good thing he lived alone, he guessed, and didn't have to convince someone to let him keep all of it.

That was the only good part of it, he admitted. As he'd packed away his room, he knew Paige was in the school auditorium, probably accepting her new job even as he put away the remains of his old one. He would miss his teaching position at Peach Leaf Elementary, but now he could focus completely on art therapy, just like he'd always wanted, and he could earn his doctorate at the same time. He wondered what his father would think of the degree. It was probably useless to the old man because it wasn't an

MBA, but still, the young boy in him longed to share his news with his dad. Even after all these years, he still ached to repair the broken relationship, but time hadn't taught him any more about how to do it.

His heart broke to think of just seeing Paige around town. She had never wanted anyone to know they were together, but it would only be worse now that there was little possibility of her ever seeing reason. Part of him wanted to run into the auditorium and tell her how he felt, but he knew she would hate it if he did that, and he would lose any chance of her ever wanting to make a go of it. She had to come to it on her own terms.

"Liam."

He sucked in a breath of surprise as he turned to see Paige standing in the doorway. He hadn't heard her open it. She was gorgeous in a navy dress, sexier than anything he'd ever seen her wear. Her hair fell in waves around her shoulders, natural the way he liked it, and her makeup was subtle and tasteful, enhancing her incredible beauty. He blinked at her, at a loss for words. There was nothing more he could say or do to make her understand that he loved her, aside from shouting it out loud, which was precisely what she did not want. He had grown to feel more for her than he ever had with Callie. Paige's courage and drive challenged him and made him want to push back to get her to be herself. He didn't know what he would do without her, but he was no stranger to the way he felt when she denied her real feelings. When she'd fought with him at the ice cream shop about the

Realtor knowing they were dating, he'd gone straight back to the way he'd felt when Callie had told him she couldn't be with him if he wouldn't give up the idea of having kids. The two circumstances were worlds apart, but he couldn't stand to have Paige feel shame in being with him.

"Liam, we need to talk."

Chapter Eleven

"There's nothing more to say, Paige. You made it fairly clear that you're not interested in showing people how you feel about me. How am I supposed to believe that you feel anything for me when you refuse to acknowledge it in public?" The blow wasn't fair and he knew it. He knew perfectly well that she hid her feelings because of their jobs, but he needed to know how she really felt and that to not be a factor in their relationship.

Paige looked as though he'd slapped her. Seeing her wounded face, he supposed he may as well have.

"You know it's not like that."

"Then how is it, Paige? Because how it feels is that you're ashamed to be seen with me. And I'm beginning to wonder if it's really because of your job."

She opened her mouth and shut it again into a hard angry line. "You know the cost of people seeing us together. Don't you worry about losing your job?"

Now was his chance to tell her. He could just tell her that he'd been hired by the hospital and make everything okay as he longed to do. It would make the hurt disappear from her face. Wouldn't it? How could he be sure? With Callie, he'd believed the entire time they were together that she'd loved him as she said she did, and that their love was unconditional. But his desire to start a family had been enough to change her mind about spending a lifetime together, and he'd lost her.

He refused to go through that again for any reason—couldn't go through it again, not with the way he felt about Paige. His heart beat for her with an intensity he'd never known, and he knew he'd never find again. If he couldn't be with this woman, if they couldn't build a family, then he didn't want any of it. He would make his living with his art and his therapy the way he'd always wanted to, and that would be his purpose.

"Liam, you know I care for you, but I can't risk all I've worked for…for…"

"What? For me? I get it. You don't have to say anything more. You can go back to the party, and take your new job and have everything you want."

Tears shimmered in her cobalt eyes and he had to look away to keep from running to her. Despite the frustration that seared his insides, he still wanted to comfort her. He hated hurting her, but better to do it now, before things got past the point of his control, if they hadn't already. It seemed she had a pretty damn good grip on him, and he wasn't sure he could pull his way out.

"Not everything," she said quietly, and Liam heard his own pain in her voice. Words were failing him, and he had no choice but to try. If she wanted him, she would have an opportunity to tell him now, in no uncertain terms.

He rushed forward and grabbed her, pulling her close until he could smell the jasmine of her perfume. And like that, she went soft in his arms. Even if she argued from that point on, he would know she was keeping up appearances. He looked down into the precious face he'd come to love so much. He wasn't willing to let her throw it all away out of fear. Just because she'd lost her husband, didn't mean she would lose him. He would not let their pasts ruin their future before it had even begun. Of all the losses they'd suffered so far between them, if they let this go, it would be too great to bear. He lifted her until her feet rose off the floor, holding her as close as he could, and he kissed her.

Before she could convince herself to stop him, Liam had literally swept her off her feet, and she could no more pull away than she could breathe, with his body wrapped around hers and his mouth demanding that she give in to what they both needed. She could almost feel his blood boiling beneath his skin. Her brain was fuzzy and refused to operate with any reason.

She had to get her head together and figure out how to do the right thing. Remembering where she was, she fought the urge to keep kissing Liam and suddenly pulled away. Desperate to clear her head, she backed away from him, and he let her.

"I'm sorry," she said, turning so she wouldn't have to see the wounded look in his eyes. "I shouldn't have let this happen. I knew all along I couldn't have all of it." She thought he might argue with her, and when he didn't, she was surprised to feel a deep, aching sense of disappointment.

He said nothing, just stood and stared at her. She could see that he was angry, but she fought the urge to apologize further. Maybe if he blamed her—if he hated her—it would be easier for them both. "Surely you know as well as I do that this is a mistake. It can't lead to anything good."

"No, Paige," he said, shaking his head slowly. "I can't agree with you. It absolutely could lead to something good, if you would get out of the way and just let it."

"You know that's not possible. If we…"

"If we what?" He wasn't going to make this easier for her. She supposed she deserved it. She'd agreed to bring Owen for lunch at Rachel's. She'd allowed Liam to give her son attention beyond what was required of a teacher. She hadn't stopped him when he'd carried Owen upstairs and kissed her in the darkness and stolen her heart. She was to blame for whatever consequences befell them.

"You know we can't be together," she said.

"What is it exactly that you're afraid of, Paige? Is it because of the principal job, or something else? Because I can't help how this feels. At first, I thought it was just me feeling this way, that you were this prickly, stuck-up boss and you had no interest in me. But then, spending time with you the past few weeks, I know you feel the same way, and I'll be damned if you're going to stand here and deny it. I deserve a better explanation that that."

He was right and she knew it. She struggled for words and came up empty. The nerves she'd felt at coming here today to accept her new job and the heat of his anger filling the room were too much, and her head spun as her legs threatened to buckle beneath her.

"I don't know what to say, Liam. I've had a good few weeks, a fantastic few weeks, with you, but it's Owen I'm concerned for here. I have to do what's right by him."

"And what's that?" Liam crossed his arms and stood, refusing to budge. He wasn't going to let her off the hook at all.

"I have to give him stability beyond his home and his therapy—"

"Therapy that was clearly working so well," Liam interrupted in a sarcastic tone. Paige felt anger rise up, and she was thankful for it. It made it that much easier to kick him out of her life. But when she looked up to bite back at him, she noticed his face had changed.

"I'm sorry," he said, running a hand through his hair. "I didn't mean that."

She wanted to tell him it was okay, but she didn't. The more she said, the deeper in she would be, and it would be painful enough to dig her way out from where she already was.

"I am Owen's only parent," she said, stabbing a finger into her chest. The tears she was so good at keeping inside once again pooled up behind her eyes and stung.

"I have to assure him that I will be here no matter what and that he is my priority. And I need this job, so that I can give him the best life possible."

"You've already done that, Paige. Owen has everything he needs to succeed. You've provided a life for him that most couples would struggle to give him. He has plenty of stability and plenty of love. What more could he possibly need from you?"

Paige looked down at her feet, hoping to find answers in the sparkle of her shoes. How could she explain to him how it felt, knowing that no matter what she did, no matter how she succeeded or what honors she was given, she would always have the shadow of her father over her life? To many of the townspeople, she would always be the daughter of the principal of Peach Leaf High who had had an affair with one of his teachers and wrecked his marriage to Paige's mother.

"Sometimes stability and love are simply not enough."

She could see that he didn't understand, but she didn't know how to explain it to him. "I have a lot to prove, Liam, and I am the sole provider for Owen. I can't let up or else it could all fall apart right in front of me."

Liam's expression was sad and weary-looking. Paige hated fighting with him and that she had crushed his normally upbeat demeanor out of him. Little did he know that, since he had come into her life, she was happier than she'd ever been. On some level, the newness of the feeling terrified her. Did she have a right to be happy when Mark was gone? Would Owen think that she didn't love his father anymore? Would he forget about Mark altogether?

"Paige, I understand how important Owen is to you. I get it. You don't have space in your life for another man. And I'm not Owen's father. I never will be. I can see that there's not any room for me here. So I'll make it easy for you and just go."

Say something, Paige. Make him stay. He has to stay.

But she didn't, and, standing there in silence, she lost her chance. She saw his face fall and it was like the light just went out of him. She refused to open her mouth and cause him any more pain. She remained fixed in place as he grabbed the last of his boxes and walked out the door. The finality in the click behind him brought a flood of tears. She didn't even ask him where he was going or if he would stay on for the semester. She had no right to.

In trying to shield her own, she had broken both their hearts.

Back at the dinner, looking at the chicken on her plate made Paige feel queasy despite the fact that she was starving. She looked over to the empty dinner plate beside her and pulled the full glass of wine closer to her own plate.

Luckily Cam was on the other side of her.

"You're doing fine," Cam said, reaching over to squeeze Paige's hand. "Just remember what we talked about, okay? No one's making you do this. It's your choice and your choice only."

Paige did her best version of a convincing nod. She still had no idea what she would say once she got up there. She knew that once Principal Matthews announced that Paige was taking the post after the older woman retired, the teachers would expect some sort of commentary from her about her goals and plans for the school. Just thinking about it made her insides turn to marshmallow. She would look like a deer in the headlights. Maybe that would be best anyway—if she made a complete idiot of herself, then surely no one would want her taking over the highest position at the elementary school.

Cam pulled away what was to have been Liam's glass of wine. Paige instinctively grabbed it back.

"I don't think so, sweetie. The last thing you need is too much of this stuff when you get up there." Cam pried the glass from Paige's death grip and took a long sip of the crimson liquid as she winked at Paige over the rim. "Trust me. I'm saving you a load of trouble."

She was probably right. Paige's legs felt wobbly enough as it was, and she was still seated. Imagine what would happen when she stood up and had to walk to a stage in front of hundreds of people.

She felt warmth behind her and turned, only to be disappointed at not finding Liam standing there as she'd hoped. She wasn't sure if she was strong enough yet to deal with the repercussions of people seeing them together, but she knew she would feel a lot better if he was there beside her. A couple of weeks ago she would never have believed it, but she had to admit it now. *After she had pushed him away forever.*

She needed him.

"Ms. Graham…"

She looked over her shoulder to see one of Owen's teachers, Jacey King. "Oh, hi, Jacey. Call me Paige. We're not at school."

The woman smiled. "Do you have a moment?"

"Yes, of course. Is everything okay?"

Jacey smiled again. "I just wanted to let you know how well Owen's doing in gym class." Paige felt her heart soften at the sound of her son's name. She hadn't had a chance to talk to any of Owen's teachers lately besides Liam. She knew he was speaking a little here and there, but she hadn't gotten a full update from any of them yet.

"Is he really doing better?" Paige asked, turning in her chair to face Jacey.

"Definitely," the other woman said, reaching out to touch Paige's forearm. "I'm so proud of him lately. It's almost as if he just got better overnight. I couldn't believe it the first time he talked to a neighbor. The kids were playing soccer and he asked Timothy Simons to pass the ball, just like that, as if he'd done it this year a million times before."

Paige bit her lip as her sadness over Liam crashed into her joy at Owen's achievement. It was what she'd wanted for him, and all of a sudden, there it was. It seemed so simple.

"I'm so glad to hear that."

"Is it the therapy that's helping so much?"

"Yes, I think so," Paige answered. Not exactly a lie. It was Liam's art therapy, and that alone, wasn't it. She had taken Owen to so much talk and behavior therapy over the past six months, after she'd gotten over her initial denial that anything serious was wrong, and it hadn't really helped much. She didn't blame the therapist, but something must have changed—something aside from just therapy—to make him improve so rapidly over the past couple of weeks.

"Well, I've just been glad to see it. The kids have been so calm about it. I guess they're just more accepting of things like that than me. When I heard him talk to Timothy, you could have knocked me over with a breath of air."

Liam had worked with Owen on art projects, and

she knew from his explanations that the form of therapy could be very effective, but she still couldn't quite believe how quickly Owen had gotten better. He'd become close friends with Jeremy and Kaylie and spent time regularly with them, and Paige had watched him go from saying a couple of words to having completely normal conversations for a child his age.

"Thanks so much for telling me, Jacey. It means the world to me to hear that." Jacey patted Paige's shoulder and walked back to her own table.

It dawned on her then, the truth that had been right in front of her the whole time.

Owen's progress was directly parallel to her relationship to Liam. As she and Liam had grown closer, and as the three of them had spent more time together, Owen's conversation had become more and more fluid and frequent. She thought of the three of them laughing together as they'd watched movies, and how Liam had tucked Owen in and read the boy's favorite stories over and over the couple of times he'd stayed late, never tiring of the same ones even when Owen wanted to hear them ten times in a row. She thought of the day they had gone to look at houses for Liam, and how happy they had all been before they'd run into Principal Matthews's husband—until she had panicked and ran scared. She felt an ache form in her empty stomach, and it spread slowly to her heart.

Owen had gotten better because she had gotten better. There was no other explanation. All the ther-

apy in the world wouldn't have done him any good if
she had remained stagnant. He had been able to open
his heart because Paige had opened hers.

She finally understood. Owen didn't need for
her to get the principal job. He didn't need her to
have more money for additional therapy sessions in
order to get better. He'd started to heal because she
had done so—or at least she had started to. If Owen
was doing so well with her having been only half-
willing to let Liam work his magic, then she could
only imagine how well her son would do if she were
truly able to admit her feelings for Liam and let him
into their lives permanently.

Owen had all he needed. *She* was the one who
hadn't realized it yet.

Paige suddenly became very aware that all eyes
were on the front of the room at the stage area. She
looked up to see Principal Matthews onstage, speaking into the microphone. All moisture left Paige's
mouth and she felt her body go cold even before
she could make out the fuzzy words coming from
her boss.

"You all know this woman in her role as our assistant principal, and she's been a priceless asset to the
school over the past few years. She's made incredible improvements to our kids' programs and she's
been amazing on the office side of things, as well.
Every parent I've spoken to about her adores her and
admires her work with our children. They're the reason we go to work every day, and Ms. Graham was
an award-winning teacher, so she's got the experi-

ence and the talent to make even more of a mark at our school. So, without further ado, would you all help me to welcome the newest principal of Peach Leaf…Ms. Paige Graham."

Paige tried to move, but she was frozen in her chair. She felt Cam's elbow in her side and she looked at her best friend.

"I can't do this," she said. "Go up there for me?"

Cam shook her head no. "You can do this, and you will. You're ready and you're strong enough. Just go up there, make a quick statement and then tell her how you feel when you get a chance."

Paige became suddenly and horribly aware that all eyes in the room had focused on her. She pulled one leg out from under the table and grabbed Cam's hand to steady herself.

"You're okay. You've got this."

Paige finally gained enough footing to make her way to the stage, hoping the whole way she wouldn't topple over because of her clumsiness caused by her nervousness combined with the height of her heels.

When she got to the stage, Principal Matthews was standing at the microphone, an enormous smile covering her face. How could she let her boss down like this? Ms. Matthews would never forgive her. She was about to look like a fool in front of the entirety of Peach Leaf Elementary. She let her boss embrace her and then the principal stepped a few feet away. Paige took the microphone in her hands and it greeted her with a terrible screeching noise. Luckily, everyone in the room laughed rather than groaned, but the sound of it did nothing to calm her nerves. She found Cam's face at their table and latched onto her best friend's eyes.

Cam mouthed the words "You can do this" over and over again. She even gave a little thumbs-up.

As glad as Paige was for the vote of confidence, she needed to see Liam's face there. She had to have his strength to supplement her own so that she could tell the truth and get it over with. For what felt like the first time in who knew how long, she wasn't concerned with what anyone else thought. She just wanted to say what was in her heart. The weight of everything pressed down on her, and she felt heavy with the responsibility of it all. She was tired of running to be the best mom and the best at her job. She had done enough. Now, it was time to do something for herself.

"Thank you all so much for coming," she said into the microphone. "I can't say how honored I am to have been offered this job. Principal Matthews will be greatly missed." Page looked behind her and saw her boss wipe a tear from her eye. "I've lived here my entire life. In fact, as you may know, I went to Peach Leaf Elementary. I've lived here my whole life." She saw discomfort in several of her colleagues' eyes as she avoided talking about her father, but she kept going. "I love teaching, and I love the kids more than I can say. And as I said, I am so grateful to have been considered for this position." She saw some confused looks sweep the room.

Here goes. "But as much as I love it all, I'm afraid I can't accept this job."

Quiet gasps rippled like waves throughout the audience.

Paige swallowed and closed her eyes. She could do this. She turned and faced Ms. Matthews. "I'm so sorry," she said. She couldn't tell what the older woman was feeling, but she continued anyway. "I'm not right for the job."

Ms. Matthews wore a look of perplexity. "But I don't understand. You're the best person for it. You… you're perfect for it."

Paige took both of Ms. Matthews's hands in her own and looked into her eyes. "I may be perfect for it, but it's not perfect for me. I'm so sorry. I just want to go back to teaching. I can't do this."

"But…"

"I have to go now." Paige made her way down the stairs at the side of the stage and walked back through the tables, careful not to meet anyone's eyes. She kept her focus on the doorway out, on Owen and on the life she knew she wanted.

She had to find Liam. She ran as fast as she could down the hallway and out the door, hoping stupidly that she might catch him before he left completely. She had seen several other boxes in the room after he'd left, and she knew he would have had to go back for them. Her heels clicked violently along the floor of the empty hallway, the noise shattering any shred of calm she had left. Her heart still pounded from the way everyone had stared at her as she'd run from the auditorium, wondering what in the world had happened to her, probably thinking she had lost her mind. She couldn't worry about that now. Now the only thing that mattered was finding Liam and telling him how she really felt.

When she got to the classroom, she put a hand on the door and let it linger there, afraid to turn the knob. When she finally did, only emptiness greeted her.

She didn't know how long she'd sat there when she heard a voice calling her from down the hall. She'd slunk down on the floor and remained there, unable to move. The door opened slowly and she saw Cam come in, her face scared and confused. They looked across the room at each other, the silence saying everything. Paige looked down into her lap.

"He's gone."

Chapter Twelve

Owen's excitement was palpable from the backseat as Paige pulled up to the school. He was ready for Parents' Night; it was all he'd talked about for weeks, and he had practiced his lines so many times that Paige knew the skit by heart. "You know what they say when an actor goes on stage, sweetie?"

"What, Mom?"

"They never say, 'Good luck.' It's bad luck to say 'good luck' to an actor."

Owen giggled. "How can it be bad luck to say 'good luck' when 'good luck' means you're supposed to have good luck?" Paige turned and looked at him in the backseat and they both laughed at the silliness of it. Her son's resilient positivity had kept her heart beating since the night of the dinner a couple of weeks ago.

"I have no idea. We should look it up when we get home. I just know that instead of 'good luck,' they always say 'break a leg.'"

Owen's eyes widened. "I definitely don't want that to happen."

"You and me both, kiddo," Paige said as she got out and helped Owen out of the car. He looked great in his costume. All the kids were supposed to come dressed as school supplies to welcome the parents. Owen was dressed as an eraser. He looked ridiculous and cute and Paige had to smile each time she saw the gigantic pink rectangle. Owen didn't seem to mind being dressed up like an office supply. He was just happy to be going onstage with the rest of his class. On some level, Paige thought he knew how important it was that he had speaking lines. Even though they hadn't sat down to talk about it, mostly because she was afraid to question a good thing when she saw it, she knew he had to be aware of the significance of his accomplishments over the past few weeks.

But that wasn't the only thing she had avoided talking about.

"This way, Mom," Owen said, leading her through the front doors and down a hallway to the auditorium where the first-grade class was supposed to meet backstage.

She had avoided saying much about Liam. She knew Owen felt his absence; he asked about his teacher almost every day. She was just glad that she hadn't let Owen know too much about the relationship so that he didn't expect more. He clearly missed Liam, but she had told her son only that Mr. Campbell was out of town for a few weeks, and she wasn't sure if he would be coming back. After being glum for a few days, Owen had seemed to perk back up. She had Liam to thank for that. He had never made a big deal out of Owen's talking, so Owen didn't associate it with his presence and had been able to keep on going when his teacher had gone. Liam had been right about that. He had been right about a lot of things.

Part of her hoped, by some chance, that she might see him around town, but she wasn't even sure if he was still living in Peach Leaf, and she'd been too afraid to ask Rachel if he had moved away. All she knew was that he'd resigned from his teaching position and had recommended someone who had been hired in his place.

She knew she owed him an apology, and so much more, but she needed to give him time. She had hurt him enough already. But God, she missed him. He brought so much light into their lives, and though she tried to stay upbeat to keep her son happy, she was struggling with the darkness in Liam's absence.

They met with Cam backstage and Paige offered to help. Her best friend's red hair was wild and her eyes were darting every which way as she clamored to get all of the kids in line. Paige shouted at Cam through the ruckus to let her know if she needed anything and Cam grinned at her over Owen's head. She gave a thumbs-up, pointing to an assistant teacher nearby, and Paige felt a little bit better knowing things weren't as bad as they seemed. Kids were running around all over the place, but it looked like at least they were all dressed. Child-size pens and pencils were everywhere, along with a few juice-smeared faces and some hair-pulling. Paige wiped some mouths and stopped a few minor catastrophes before heading out to the audience.

She found a seat near the back. After what had happened at Principal Matthews's dinner, she wasn't exactly dashing to mingle. Her boss had taken it well after the initial shock, and Paige found out a week later that another senior teacher had been offered the position—a good choice—and she'd been able to rest a bit, knowing that she was off the hook. She'd mourned for a day or two over the lost opportunity and then had decided she liked having the pressure gone. Her time with Owen was more relaxed and she was better able to concentrate on each moment they spent together. They'd gone to movies, the park and swimming at the local pool more times in the past week than they had in the entire last year and this year combined. She enjoyed it so much that she was seriously considering going back to teaching and giving up her job as assistant principal altogether, but her boss had had enough lately, and Paige would save that news for after the end of the semester. She looked forward to spending her days in a classroom again.

She settled into her seat and looked around her before the lights dimmed. It was a great turnout. In the back of her mind, she had to admit that there was still a hint of fear that Owen might freeze up and not be able to say his lines. She had thought about sitting up front so he could see her well, but then she'd decided against it. If he could look out into the audience and forget himself, then he had a better chance of not panicking.

The lights started to dim and Paige turned off her cell phone and tucked her purse under her seat. Her nerves shot up to the surface and she took several deep breaths.

Just have faith in him. He'll do fine. She heard Liam's voice in her head as she calmed herself, and the intensity of missing him flooded her body all over again. She fought back tears until she realized that no one could see them, and then she let them fall silently one by one into the darkness. How she wished Liam was there to see Owen, to be with her while she watched her son do what she had, not so long ago, thought he might never be able to do again. How she wished Liam could see what he had accomplished, what he had brought back to life.

She was surprised to find that her thoughts went first to Liam, and not to Mark. Somehow she knew that her husband would be okay with it. She knew he would want her to move on and to find someone else to love, which she had done.

That is, before she had messed it all up horribly. She wiped her eyes and bit her lip as she saw

Owen walk onstage and take his place. The next few
moments passed quickly as she mouthed her child's
lines with him. He nailed every last one without a
single mistake, though she wouldn't have cared if he
had given someone else's lines entirely. She would
have been happy all the same, just to hear his voice
up there. She clasped her hands together and pulled
them against her heart. And then, as Owen exited the
stage, her heart throbbed with sorrow again, mixed
with determination.

Suddenly it was the most important thing in the
world that she call Liam and tell him what had happened, what Owen had done. She waited on the edge
of agony until the play was over—Cam would kill
her if she found out her best friend hadn't watched
the whole of it—and then as the crowd burst into up-
roarious applause, she rose from her seat and made
a beeline for the lobby. She dug around in the bottom of her purse, cursing as she grasped in vain for
her phone, and finally she grabbed the hard plastic
in her fingers. She pulled it out as though it were a
hot coal and waited for it to wake up again. Dialing
Liam's number while keeping an eye out for Owen
to come out from backstage with the rest of the cast,
she waited with bated breath as she heard the first
ring. As the audience began to file out of the auditorium, she lost the call. She managed to find a corner and dialed again. In the distance a phone rang
parallel to her dial tone.

It couldn't be. There had to be a million phones

in the place and one of them had just coincidentally synced up with her call.

"Hello." The voice was in her ear and also…a few feet away where the ringing had been a minute before. No way.

"Liam."

"Paige."

She followed the real voice rather than the one in her ear and found him. They stood facing each other. He was even more handsome than he had been in the memories she'd carried around for the past few weeks. His hair was slightly shorter, but still tousled and sexy, and his eyes were the same intense green she remembered.

Her heart pounded in her ears and for a long moment, they just stood there staring at each other, phones in ears, until she burst out laughing at how silly they must look. She put her phone away and Liam pulled his down from his ear. And then he reached out and pulled her into his arms. He held her out from him so he could see her face and she smiled into his face to let him know how glad she was to see him.

And then she did what she should have done two weeks ago, when she'd stood with him in the classroom before she'd finally made up her mind and had chosen to do what she needed rather than what she thought she should do for a hoard of reasons that weren't nearly as important.

"I'm so sorry," she said, and he shook his head

as though she didn't need to apologize. But she did, and they both knew it.

"I should have told you to stay. I should have figured it out sooner and told you how I felt so you wouldn't leave."

"I'm here now," he said, pulling her closer. "And I'm not going anywhere."

"I was so worried about all the wrong things. I couldn't see what was right in front of me. You were right the whole time and..."

"And I'm sorry I didn't fight you harder, Paige, but I knew you had to figure it out on your own. You didn't need me for that, but I didn't want to start a life with you until you were absolutely ready for one. I needed to know that you were ready for me. But I also want you to know that it's okay for you to keep Mark alive for Owen. He needs that, and I'll help you do it. There's no need for him to forget his dad."

Paige's heart swelled with all the words she'd longed to hear. He was really here to stay. And she was willing to do whatever it took to keep him.

"I'm going back to teaching," she said, hoping to see his face light up with the news. It would mean they could be together without worrying what anyone thought. They would be equals in the school with her no longer in a supervisory role. She would have no power to show favoritism and worry constantly about being reprimanded for rewarding him, which she knew she would have to do at some point because he was, without argument, an extraordinary teacher.

Instead of delight, she saw something else. Something she couldn't quite identify.

"That won't be necessary, Paige, unless you want to do it just for you."

"What do you mean?"

"I've been offered a full-time position as an art therapist at Peach Leaf Memorial. I'm going to have my own program and classroom, and they're even willing to fund the remaining classes that I need to complete my doctorate." The pure joy in his eyes made her own heart swell near to bursting with matched emotion. She couldn't believe it.

"Why didn't you tell me?" She couldn't help but feel slightly wounded, but whatever he said, she knew he would have had a good reason for withholding the information from her.

"Because when I found out about it, it wasn't a sure thing yet. I took a week off from teaching to meet with the hospital director and some other staff to see if it would really work. I had to compile a lot of research from my experiences and put together several presentations. It was pretty brutal, actually, but the director believed in the idea and wanted me to make the same impression on the rest of the board. They loved all of it. The research doesn't lie about the effectiveness of art therapy, and I've worked with enough students that I knew I could prove it would help so many people in the hospital. And...there was something else. I needed to give you some time to work things out on your own. I couldn't be the one to tell you if you were ready to make a go at this or not, and I didn't want your decision to be clouded with anything—the school, your boss, Mark or even Owen. I needed to know if you felt the same way I do—just you."

She stared into those evergreen eyes and saw a future there with him. A future she would do anything for now. And she jumped in.

"I love you, Liam Campbell, and I am so glad you're here." And with that, she kissed him in front of the entire staff of Peach Leaf Elementary and a hundred or more parents. And she didn't mind a single shred what any of them thought. She forgot her father, the principal job and everything else as she gave Liam every part of her. When they pulled apart she saw Cam out of the corner of her eye, and her best friend winked from across the room.

"Mr. Campbell!"

"What on earth?" Liam asked, beaming as a giant eraser hurtled toward them.

"You're back!" Owen ran up and hugged Liam with epic force, pushing him even closer to Paige. Owen looked up at both of them, a huge grin plastered across his face. Liam reached down to hug Owen, and the three of them were wrapped into a family embrace.

"Does this mean you're going to come live with us?" Owen asked, and Paige blushed.

"Well, I was actually hoping that you might come and live with me," Liam said, "but we'll have to run it by your mom first because she might want to come along too." Love filled Liam's eyes as he grinned at her over Owen's head. "I've bought a house, and I think you'll absolutely adore it," he said to her. "And of course there's a pool in the backyard and a room for Owen, if you'll say yes."

Paige took a deep breath, and with certainty, she answered, "Yes." She let him lift her off the floor then and didn't care who saw her as the art teacher pulled her in for another kiss. It felt so good to do what made her happy, and kissing Liam was at the top of the list.

"Would the two of you join me for dinner then?" Liam asked. "I know where we can find a great hamburger and some ice cream for dessert." Owen agreed enthusiastically, and the three of them walked out of the school hand in hand.

Epilogue

One year later

Liam stood at the back of their house on the top step of the freshly stained, gleaming deck. He looked up as she began her walk through the yard, and the tears he'd sworn to himself he'd keep away pinched at his eyes and nose.

Paige was dressed in a knee-length pale yellow summer gown, her feet bare in the soft dewy morning grass of their yard. She mirrored the sunshine that came from the sky and glinted off her hair. There were hardly any tears as she walked toward him; her face was filled with only hope and happiness, and Liam had everything he needed right there, with her and Owen. When she reached where he stood, he held out his hands and squeezed hers in them, his skin tingling with their touch and the anticipation of sharing his life with her.

The minister said his part and when it was time for the rings, they turned to watch Owen make his way up the aisle, looking ever the handsome young man in his small tuxedo, with a butter-yellow rose pinned to his little chest. The boy grinned as he passed their few guests—Cam winked at him, and Paige's sister, Emily, burst into happy tears at the sight of her nephew. The boy they'd all been so worried about not that long ago. The boy who was now thriving at school, playing Little League baseball with his friends and talking like a chatterbox to anyone who'd lend him an ear.

Liam's family was beautiful, and he couldn't wait to start the rest of his life with them. He had left Peach Leaf Elementary and started full-time a week later at Peach Leaf Memorial, where he now spent his days helping kids like Owen. Sometimes he even brought Owen up to help him, along with their new family member, a rescue dog they'd chosen and trained together for service but who had quickly become Owen's best bud. The kid had a calm, mature demeanor and Liam's patients responded well to having Owen in the room. He gave them hope that they, too, would get better.

Liam had purchased the house before he'd gone to see Owen's skit that night, knowing full well he would have to back out of the contract if Paige didn't want to share it with him, but he'd had a feeling she would. So he'd put all his eggs in that one, fragile basket and thanked his lucky stars when she'd said yes to being his forever.

The house was perfect. It had a giant kitchen where they spent evenings cooking together, sometimes even with Owen, and a living room large enough for the three of them and Rachel's family to spread out with a board game. Owen had picked his room immediately—a second-story bedroom with a window seat where he could spend afternoons reading or drawing, which he'd grown increasingly fond of and was getting quite good at.

When Paige became pregnant a few weeks before the wedding, she told the new principal that she wouldn't be coming back the following semester, and Liam supported her decision. He knew she'd always wanted to spend more time with Owen, and now she would be able to stay home with her son in the summers and spend her days with the new baby. His heart overflowed at his good fortune.

As he slipped the ring on her finger, he thought of the tiny life growing inside her and hoped the baby would have the best of both of them—his passion and Paige's determined strength. And mostly he hoped their child would have their combined bravery and never let fear get in the way of trying again, even when the world had knocked him or her down.

If he had to pick one thing he'd learned from Paige and Owen to share with their new little one, he would tell their child that love was worth risking everything for, especially when it was for forever.

* * * * *

COMING NEXT MONTH FROM

HARLEQUIN°

SPECIAL EDITION

Available September 23, 2014

#2359 TEXAS BORN • by Diana Palmer
Michelle Godfrey might be young, but she's fallen hard for Gabriel Brandon, the rugged rancher who rescued her from a broken home. Over time, their bond grows, and Gabriel eventually realizes there's more to his affection than just a protective instinct. But Michelle stumbles on Gabriel's deepest secrets, putting their lives—and their love—in jeopardy.

#2360 THE EARL'S PREGNANT BRIDE
The Bravo Royales • by Christine Rimmer
Genevra Bravo-Calabretti might be a princess of Montedoro, but that doesn't mean she doesn't make mistakes. When one night hard with the devilishly handsome Rafael DeValery, Earl of Hartmore, results in a surprise pregnancy, Genny can't believe it. Meanwhile, Rafe is determined to make her his bride. Will the fairy-tale couple get a happily-ever-after of their own?

#2361 THE LAST-CHANCE MAVERICK
Montana Mavericks: 20 Years in the Saddle! • by Christyne Butler
Vanessa Brent might be a famous artist, but not even she can paint a happy ending for her best friend. Following her late BFF's instructions, Vanessa moves to Rust Creek Falls to find true happiness, which is where she meets architect Jonah Dalton. He's looking to rebuild his own life after a painful divorce, but little does each know that the other might be the key to true love.

#2362 DIAMOND IN THE RUFF
Matchmaking Mamas • by Marie Ferrarella
Pastry chef Lily Langtry can whip up delicious desserts with ease...but finding a boyfriend? That's a bit harder. The Matchmaking Mamas decide to take matters into their own hands and gift Lily with an adorable puppy that needs some extra TLC—from handsome veterinarian Dr. Christopher Whitman! Can the canine bring together Lily and Christopher in a *paws*-itively perfect romance?

#2363 THE RANCHER WHO TOOK HER IN
The Bachelors of Blackwater Lake • by Teresa Southwick
Kate Scott is a bride on the lam when she shows up at Cabot Dixon's Montana ranch. Her commitment-shy host is still reeling from his wife's abandonment of their family. But Cabot's son, Tyler, decides that Kate is going to be his new mom, and his dad can't help but be intrigued by Blackwater Lake's latest addition. Will Kate and Cabot each get a second chance at a happy ending?

#2364 ONE NIGHT WITH THE BEST MAN • by Amanda Berry
Ever since the end of her relationship with Dr. Luke Ward, Penny Montgomery has said "no" to long-term love. But seeing Luke again changes everything. He's the best man at his brother's wedding, and maid of honor Penny is determined to rekindle the sparks with her former flame, but just temporarily. However, love doesn't always follow the rules.... _____

YOU CAN FIND MORE INFORMATION ON UPCOMING HARLEQUIN° TITLES, FREE EXCERPTS AND MORE AT WWW.HARLEQUIN.COM.

HSECNM0914

SPECIAL EXCERPT FROM

H HARLEQUIN®

SPECIAL EDITION

Enjoy this sneak peek from New York Times *bestselling
author Diana Palmer's TEXAS BORN, the latest in*
THE LONG, TALL TEXANS *miniseries.*

*Forced from her home by her cruel stepmother,
Michelle Godfrey is out of luck...until Gabriel Brandon
comes to her rescue. The tall, brooding cowboy is
devilishly handsome, but he's her guardian—and
nothing more. As Michelle grows into the woman she's
always wanted to be, can the shy beauty show Gabriel
that* she's *the only one he needs?*

***

Just for an instant, Gabriel worried about putting Michelle
in the line of fire, considering his line of work. He had
enemies. Dangerous enemies who wouldn't hesitate to
threaten anyone close to him. Of course, there was his
sister, Sara, but she'd lived in Wyoming for the past few
years, away from him, on a ranch they co-owned. Now he
was putting her in jeopardy along with Michelle.

But what could he do? The child had nobody. Now that
her idiot stepmother, Roberta, was dead, Michelle was truly
on her own. It was dangerous for a young woman to live
alone, even in a small community. And there was also the
question of Roberta's boyfriend, Bert.

Gabriel knew things about the man that he wasn't eager to share with Michelle. Bert was part of a criminal organization, and he knew Michelle's habits. He also had a yen for her, if what Michelle had blurted out to Gabriel once was true—and he had no indication that she would lie about it. Bert might decide to come try his luck with her now that her stepmother was out of the picture. That couldn't be allowed.

Gabriel was surprised by his own affection for Michelle. It wasn't paternal. She was, of course, far too young for anything heavy. She was a beauty, kind and generous and sweet. She was the sort of woman he usually ran from. No, strike that, she was no woman. She was still unfledged, a dove without flight feathers. He had to keep his interest hidden. At least, until she was grown up enough that it wouldn't hurt his conscience to pursue her. Afterward…well, who knew the future?

***

Don't miss TEXAS BORN
by New York Times *bestselling author Diana Palmer,*
the latest installment in
THE LONG, TALL TEXANS *miniseries.*

Available October 2014 wherever
Harlequin® Special Edition books and ebooks are sold.

♦ HARLEQUIN®

SPECIAL EDITION

Life, Love and Family

Coming in October 2014
THE EARL'S PREGNANT BRIDE
by *NEW YORK TIMES* bestselling author
Christine Rimmer

Genevra Bravo-Calabretti might be a princess of
Montedoro, but that doesn't mean she's doesn't
make mistakes. When one night with the devilishly
handsome Rafael DeValery, Earl of Hartmore,
results in a surprise pregnancy, Genny can't believe
it. Meanwhile, Rafe is determined to make her
his bride. Will the fairy-tale couple get a
happily-ever-after of their very own?

Don't miss the latest edition of
THE BRAVO ROYALES *continuity!*

Available wherever books and ebooks are sold!

HSE65842